WALKING ON STONES

Notes from the End of the Twentieth Century

Rayne Corbin

Copyright © 2021 Rayne Corbin

All rights reserved

The characters and events portrayed in this book are fictitious. Any similarity to real persons, living or dead, is coincidental and not intended by the author.

No part of this book may be reproduced, or stored in a retrieval system, or transmitted in any form or by any means, electronic, mechanical, photocopying, recording, or otherwise, without express written permission of the publisher.

ISBN-13: 979-8705413058

Cover Design: Rayne Corbin

CONTENTS

Title Page
Copyright
Walking on Stones
Chapter 1: Finding the Mountains   1
Chapter 2: Meandering Path to Nowhere   39
Chapter 3: Dead-End Platform   76
Chapter 4: Antiquated Beach   115
Chapter 5: Walking on Stones   165
Chapter 6: Synchronizing Fates   204
About The Author   243
Books By This Author   245

WALKING ON STONES

RAYNE CORBIN

CHAPTER 1: FINDING THE MOUNTAINS

The fleeting moment Sela feels the rocky floor of the isolated beach beneath her feet, newly seeing it for the first instance as she did countless times during her youth, she is instantly hindered by an overwhelming, recurring impression of coinciding past and present experiences. Her enthusiasms quietly overcome her while an unknowingly impending future curls the opposing sides into a recognizable, changeless moment of focalized familiarity at her return. She feels she has lived many times before this instant placing her here now once again, and the same reoccurring, conflicted involvement between herself and the events of her life leading her back to this beach.

Sometimes, she discovers such overlapping moments surrounding her, as if the seemingly normal, binding constraints between past, present, and future cease to exist as an apparent flowing deliberation, and instead the three tenses occur as a single collective, like a still pond her awareness traverses solely on the threshold of its absorbing and reflecting surface, its limiting thinness the summit of her fathomability; and afterwards, reflecting upon specific events, no other explanation could possess her mind other than to have lived it before, by every possible choice accorded to every possible outcome. Somewhere within that infinity of alternatives she can look up at any moment and find herself there, within a location, a seeming time, caught by some occurring events reducing her to one of an immeasurable, connected with those preceding it and others still to come. The deep depths below her surfacing awareness and the colorful, dimensional world encompassing her hold the innumerable prior choices already satisfied beyond her skill to fully chase in entirety, of a world of her making but also freely accessible as a risky making of immeasurable outcomes for others still to be found in endless repetition.

In its way, it seems a futile and pointless approach to unearthing the meaning or make-up behind reality, of looking at yourself within a capturing, undefining moment and being counted as a part of it: believing in the moment as a crest of cautionary existence, as if that is all there is, the moment, the fixed present in utter correction, in any direction she looks and every chance she decides to risk.

Still, so long as the instants of imposing awareness persist, she believes she is following the correct path of her choosing, unearthing within present moments the markers of the formerly laid future of her past, finding *now* what she has sought before during younger variations of herself also existing in the fused networks of the same matted reality no different than the one she enters on her return to the beach.

Coming back here again, indulging the close sense of overwhelming harmony of the shoreline through the grinding sounds of the stones beneath her first footstep, a sweet bitterness filling her lungs, the usual cool ocean winds of early June moistening her face, the sound of waves repeatedly melting on the pebbles of the shoreline, and witnessing as an awareness of return her place within the interrelationship, there are events and memories connecting with this moment which are not the paths of her choosing, ones precedingly forced upon her she would not prefer as the context of return to the home of her youth, and most prominently, forcing her initial reluctance at experiencing again, through the old familiar crushing of the stones beneath her footsteps, this seclusive beach.

Finally, after three years away, she has found the will and compulsion of coming back to divulge and thereby rid herself of the confounding memories of her past in its connection to this place, to the rustic home hidden within the trees behind her, back following the path which brought her here to this beach with its recurring connotations patterned to her thoughts, feelings, and memories, and her inability to continue to live without a final resolution to the inexplicable events bound to her inner being, permanently connected with this pebbled ocean shoreline and the blood-besmirch images her memories retain as a diminishing correlation.

~~

In late April, intending on getting out of the city, Sela drove away with Josh to the mountains for a week together. Recently finished with a large work-related project occupying her attentions for more than a year, and neatly tying the ends of strings for the job she recently quit for whomever came after her next to do it, she needed to get out of the city's industrial vapor and back in a vicinity to nature she hadn't closely seen or felt in a long time.

It had been three years since she last left the city, as if stranded or taking refuge there. It was an escape to the city then. She needed the balance and seeming order of synthetic structures, symbols, and meanings to surround her, and a blurred, glowing night sky. She had taken pride in busily working, the straight lines and familiar angles of the city's design soothing to her, its lighted signals and warning signages a safer path of chance for the moment: meaning, as she recognized, the future was lingering in front of her as an uncertain anticipation. To her belief, she shouldn't have to exist in mistrust of things yet to occur, to have to plan and scheme a safely future path.

Everything was routine in the city, with enough order to manage and safeguard its inhabitants including Sela. She hadn't sought its protection beforehand: such a type of anonymity as disappearing within a mass of activity. It had seemed a faint-hearted choice to seriously consider, not a quality she thought within her repertoire until it forced its possession of her, and she couldn't rid the idea of her own vulnerability from her usual self-awarenesses.

She came back to the city to overcome a fear to own her, seeking a type of peace of mind she hadn't previously considered available in such dismal, bright-lit places. She knew she risked losing a private balance the longer she stayed within its influence and enticing sights.

She had lived and studied in the city before that too; once that was completed, she hadn't intended on returning. Events changed her choices and she fled back to a secured life a city afforded her, with Josh becoming a contact and current extension of that normalized comfort she looked for in her life.

Leaving the core, through the suburbs, beyond the city's limit was a gathering release and growing loss of memory for Sela, the littering of past endurances and mindful stresses. She was excited to get away, watching the slow advance of hills and trees occupying former visions of open fields and committed homesteads. She didn't want to have to think about anything specific, looking for just a freedom of mind.

She savored the idea of leaving the city and predicted a week of emotional reconnection. Nature always made her rekindle her fondness for home, and home reminded her of herself with the attached memories stirred back to life through nature's inexhaustible array of budding moments to connect with, through the experience and growing awarenesses its wonder allowed when surrounding her in coincidences sensually close and wildly uncoverable.

The city had an ever-changeable, self-sustained mood of its own perpetrated and influenced through the mutually driven choices of its inhabitants. Mostly, what she disliked about the city was its influence on her humors, thoughts, and feelings. Being in such proximity to others so much and so often, she felt a part was lost with each new encounter, problem, or conflict. But, until she could come up with something better, it was the statistical safety in numbers Sela self-admittedly savored, and most looked for as a sense of well-being.

She found that living in the city removed

an aspect she missed: the venerable aura of things, its impression reflected from natural settings, its atmosphere of calm even at its most fierce, a practiced venerability earned through eons of toil and mistakes, an impression cast from mountains, to be found and touched in ocean settings, forests and waters; but only when you choose to look and find it beyond its obvious appeal, for otherwise it existed solely as a mutual unawareness.

She enjoyed the mountains, not having experienced being within such intermixed, immense age exposed for observation and recognition, reflected from the surfaces of rocks, eroded formations and patterns, the cresting, skyward-reaching mountain peaks structured as a relinquishing force to the counteracting plunging squeeze forcing its enormity to lazily crush into fertile dust with the subtlest of effortlessness.

The ocean and coast equally showed its age, a condition of discovery magnetic in its own way, no different than the city without the venerability, but there was a newness for her to the fresh experience in the mountains away from where she had grown up.

"The mountains are a character of time," she told Josh as they saw a crevassed waterfall cascading the lengths of jagged, protruding rock, above its constant noisy interjection, thinking of few millennia ago when the spot where they stood had no forests, waterfalls, or animals, when upward from where she looked to the sky was a solid thickness of ice higher than the mountains.

"The age they reflect make them seem more real than us. It hardly happens across our lifetimes, but these mountains sprouted up through eons of barely happening occurrences, and they will crumble to dust by the same barely occurring forces to create them."

"Where does that leave us?"

"Standing here, observing it barely occur along with us."

"You make it sound insignificant."

"No, it's very beautiful and can be appreciated for its slowness too."

"So, you're saying time is slow as we look at it here displayed in this rushing, spraying waterfall?"

"I'm saying it's so slow as to be undetectable except by us observing it occur in this waterfall. And we observe it solely due to our insignificance and our accidental being in relationship to the other forces around us."

"Then how do we see it?"

"Yes, how do we see it?"

They left the ageless rhetorical questions unanswered for the waterfall to further muse.

Sela considered time in its abstract, as a trait, a mechanism of life to better survive, much like feeling. It was what living beings learned to see, or were made or designed to see, and it texturized something different for everyone and every being caught in its waves.

In the flow of water, it was the observation of gravity, in the trees, the moments of breaking leaves, the motional spin of hardly considered energies creating a semblance of night and day, the requirement of light to travel and seek out a rapt, absorbing being, and as means to hold the past as an awareness in the present and future.

She imagined time unmistakably in nature, and with each moment, event or space, its peculiar, observable feeling intermixed with those of living others occurring in the localized moment, event and space: a feeling inseparable from any concept of time in its coinciding, practical use of mutual advantage in avoiding having to closely shoulder the sun to not be late.

In nature too, such pinpointing focus of time was lethally manipulated as the greedy chase of survival between predators and prey.

"How can the world be different for each person? Them over there," indicating an approaching man and woman following the worn path they had recently followed getting there, "they belong to a different world than us?"

"We are all made for observing the same world, but they live in a world far removed from us, and me from you, and that crow in the tree over there, and these ants on the ground, each in its own world."

"But we share the same world."

"The worlds do resemble each other."

Sela thought that as much as anyone had learned to understand it from a vantage or a lofty, insightful approach throughout history, the ability to share in its belief was sadly missing from the world of humanity by her witness of it. The empathy to understand was missing. "You know, I sometimes think, it may not be us perceiving it all so much as us making our own perception of it, or our realized agreement of perception as the predatory battle of wills."

She thought it had gone on for so long, over so many millennia, no one any longer appreciated our own part in it. Everyone thought of their own inner worlds in the context of an externally bound world fixed in time, complicated by the ceaseless events and heaving emotions resulting from the natural condition of finding the paths to disagreement as the methods of solutions, thereby making of the world a backdrop of ever-revolving conflict and appeasement in eternal cycle.

~~

At night, under the dark sky and thick torrent of stars, they sat near the provoked flames of a firepit outside a small cabin. A private, rented space under the stellar night, among shadows watchfully flittering from behind the cut edge of the near forest deep within the mountains, they comfortably sat, smoked a joint, shared a few cigarettes together, and made use of the pit's provisioning flame as a symbolic homage to primitive attentions, it's flickering display fueled by the diluted residue of stars.

For long minutes, Sela watched the fire, pondering the eons of familiarity it shared with humanity before the death of its belief as a spirit of nature. She conceived of fire as a trait of truth, reality, and of merely imaginable, vastly distant other worlds inspired by the same one frolicking with the darkness through the quenching light from the flames. Continually, the space around them consumed the tiny observable setting near the fire, in its way erasing it from the future as it tried to escape into a relative past, its hazy reflection a continually organic struggle steadily occurring between the light and its absorbed or diffused absence, a local containment enlivening the space around them. She felt this complexity as an aspect of nature easy to overlook and dismiss as ordinary rather than immensely incredible in it really happening along with her.

It wasn't the fire alone, but the entire reaction of existence happening in a small lighted sphere around them, with Sela observing it just as countless others had seen it the same, been inspired by it, protected, touched and looked for by its mere presence, old, unchanged and scattered by winds across the universe like a sparkling wildfire across a field of dried grasses, always the same flame, its dancer morphed by unseen forces deciding its animated occurrence. Its presence was undetectable and inert by whatever vigor it exerted without a mindful observer somewhere in the universe to watch it gently flicker or wildly raze, to see and worship it with awe, and to learn to perceive it with a forgetful mind.

It was only by Sela's smallness in relation to the otherwise impossibly vast that she could appreciate such an insignificant seepage of energy colorfully playing in the mountain night under the thickness of stars.

"It's hard to believe all that is real."

"All what?"

"All that up there," sweeping her arm in a dismissive gesture towards the sky, "it seems more imaginable than real."

"Imaginable? What, the universe?"

"Yeah, I mean we can't really, truly know it's there. And we wouldn't know anything we know about it if we didn't imagine it, or discovery it, another form of imagination."

"If you discover something, it is something real you discover, not something imagined."

"For something to become real, even as a value, it has to be imagined through the act of recognizing it. It could be reinterpreted that the new value of discovery only becomes real through the mindful decision to make the imaginable real, and thereby living its belief in the physical world."

"Sounds like you're trying to make the world out as our creation, only made real through us."

"Well, something had to make it, or it most likely made itself by some spark of fresh lit origin of evolvement. Besides, most of the information we know of anything comes from light, so you need to heavily trust in it to accept anything as real."

"So, you mistrust light?" Josh laughed.

"No. I'm just saying the world is a vast and impossible place, we live at a point within and atop it, equally impossibly sitting here under this immense impossibility of coincidence. All we really know is what touches us. Light from the stars is part of what touches us, only becoming real and joining with a past existence of its own through the act of us observing its energy being absorbed by us, but only inside within our minds do we really know anything we can know about the universe, it's not like a leaf we can touch with our fingers, mutually permitting the leaf to feel the strength of our outside touch in return, and it's amazingly different for each of us, and each thing within it as experience of reality."

Sela conceived that even in that difference, it was an insignificant range or vibration of reality we were experiencing. "We are trapped here on this speck of a moment and space, barely touching the surface of anything within a cosmos in which all opposites seek equilibrium in everything as a temporal achievement. It happens, we partake of it, but it goes mostly unobserved and unchallenged, even to someone within which it is widely recognized, because we believe in it," she silently finished the rest of her conversation to herself while Josh deliberated the night sky.

"So, you deny the physical for the virtual? Everything is just the imaginable made real," he later sought, still thinking about it.

"Maybe I deny nothing, perhaps that makes a difference. Or I just don't like to be fooled. When I look back, I don't want to think, *'hey, they just discovered the world is virtual, without substance or anything tangibly real, like a game,'* and then remember how I used to think it was all as real as it was obvious, nothing like what it really is, without looking any deeper." She laughed. "It could simply be me, but it all often seems very made-up. I find it hard to find distinction between the imaginable and the real, most of the time."

Once she learned something, it was hard for her to ignore it afterwards. There was no denying the truths she had fought from the world, collecting to hold them as precious objects she could share but not surrender as markers. It was her compulsive interest, distraction and the obsessed passion of an artist's intimacy which tended to primarily amalgamate her everyday reality into new days of furthering deliberations.

After a short passage in silence, she pensively continued, "I think if I had the chance to look through a large telescope at an observatory, like the most expensive ones on high mountains and far remote places looking for better darkness to track its big game celestial marvels. If the chance was offered and I was there to look at some massive thing out there like an explosive or implosive event or large-scale system like a galaxy in its entirety, with its color and potency, even if I had to fill in most of it with my imagination, I think I would cry. I know I would," as her eyes began to wet at the mere coaxing of a mental fantasy, "I'd be crying from the moment it was offered in anticipation of looking. I'd be a bit fearful of looking for not being able to take it back afterwards."

"Why would you take it back?"

"It would be like an event or moment so traumatic to a life; I'd never be able to forget or rid the image from my memory. I might become traumatized by it. It wouldn't be the same as just seeing a picture of it, something taken by someone else and handed to me as a believable reality."

A bulky sound stirred louder than it should have due to it being the quiet middle of night in the mountains: a snapping of wood closely emanated from the direction of the nearby forest's tree line. Josh stiffened upward in his seat, looking in the direction of the sound, scanning the scant available light and flickering shadows sketched by the fire and stars for the profile of anything actual.

"What are you looking for?" she calmly asked.

"I don't know. Whatever was big enough to make that sound."

"Why? Because you think it's looking for you?"

"No, but it could accidentally."

"If it wasn't for fire keeping big animals away, we wouldn't be sitting here now."

"That sounded real enough to me. I didn't imagine that!"

"Yeah, it's real. It's best not to doubt the reality of consequences. I'm just saying there are other ways of looking at things," she conceded, not wanting to lead Josh dangerously astray in the world ahead of him.

"But what's imagined here is your fear. It has nothing to do with whatever made that sound, the same as any lingering fear for something probably extremely far off by now and with no idea of you or me."

"I wasn't afraid. Just not used to it."

"There's that too. I'm the same," she confused the truth a little.

~~

They canoed the nearby lake in the early morning, gently rolling for other perspectives the unspoiled, newly reflected background angled on the prior stilled water's surface with the disfiguring waves distending in the canoe's wake. They watched with dripping paddles across their laps as the sun's light first peaked above the overhanging mountain summit, shedding the cool shadow for a vivid, warming first gaze, gradually revealing a thin lighted mist hovering above the water.

For long moments, the scene was hushed in perfect, synchronized stillness with Sela's attention. Spotting an eagle silhouetted below the crest of one of many ascending evergreens, it leapt with reaching wings and the single echoing shrill of its voice calling in reply to her sharp-eyed devotion in spotting it.

On spotting the eagle overhead sliding in their direction, Josh heavily pointed, nudging her focused attention with an indicating whisper, "eagle?"

She imagined it otherwise; with the lingering eagle above circling in mutual balance with her observation of it. She fondly recalled numerable past instances, gazing upward locked in answer to its careful returning stare while always keeping its aloofness.

In the evening, elk routinely appeared to the excitement of visitors and tourists to the local mountain village, causing mirrored conflicts of territorial aggression as the visitors braved too close. Inevitably, a spectator was seen running from charging horns to slightly escape behind a bush, a mist of dust clouded backwards from his sneakers as he slid his hurried, panicked body behind the nearest object resembling cover.

"Imagine the mind thinking getting that close to a wild animal that size is alright," sympathetic to the bluffing elk likely to take the brunt of blame and consequence should it improperly catch, maim or injure its fleeing mark.

"This is who we are as human beings now, completely lost to nature. Every new day, new people doing the same thing as the old."

"It's no good trying to talk to them."

"You'd be better off trying to reason with the elk."

"Look, the guy's heading back, slower this time, I think he took it personally with the elk. He's still moving closer."

"He's doing that for you and me and all the others watching. He won't be outdone by an animal. He'll show it who's boss, except he doesn't have a gun. I'm not sure his intimidating nature sees the difference right now."

They both regrettably laughed as the man stood in the field of dried grasses off the highway, with more cars slowing and some pulling over to see what everyone else was seeing, further increasing the enabled crowd of approaching, encircling onlookers.

The big man continued to stand his ground, bluffing the animal in challenge, three or four times his size and weight, much faster and more agile than him, and of wildly mindfulness the sole sympathy keeping the man alive, though he had no idea of it or respect for it. He slowly turned his head around, seeing with a pasted, confident smile those watching his act of bravery to his pleasant world of followers, and then returned his stare back at the animal twenty feet ahead of him, the same unknowing smile on his face, raising the small camera strung to his wrist for a picture.

"That animal could close that distance and stomp him to shreds before he had time wipe that gloat off his face. He'd die with his smile. The only thing keeping him alive is the elk can't believe another animal could be that stupid. The elk is showing great restraint, and compassion, trying to figure him out. I think it feels sorry for the man, thinks there is something wrong with him, a mental sickness or a fellow prey on last legs."

Josh laughed, "we really should yell for him to get out of there."

"We should, for the elk, but it's only likely to make a situation worse. The guy won't listen, look at him, he's moving closer, now a woman is following his lead," as the elk finally relented and began to saunter away back towards the trees.

"Besides," Sela continued, "the same thing is happening in multiple forms all over, everywhere else, in new varieties, the same thing, same impulse in denial, we shouldn't watch it anymore, it's sad to be made to view the increasing, humiliating defeat of our species. Here we are so near the turn of a millennia, and it's been two thousand years of this and worse, and that's just the years we've been really counting. Does no one alive know our age? That's all it reminds me of, and it feels like we're taking part along with everyone else, without much choice, let's move on," continuing to follow the path they were walking before being distracted by the saddening tragicomedy an aspect of humanity had provided them through a simple contact with an exposed side of nature, something beyond the crowd's comprehension or collective empathy to distinguish.

"Nature has become an amusing global zoo for entertainment as we outgrow its ranges. No need for cages anymore at this stage of our transitional journey," he enthusiastically expounded, imbued with Sela's contagious excitement, "in the end, it's all one big zoo we rudely share together."

~~

In the mornings, Sela awoke early before Josh, leaving him sleeping in his bed while she quietly made coffee for herself; the light was just beginning to slowly immerse the dimness inside the cabin, and outside the window illuminating the immeasurable, loitering changes made overnight awaiting to be held as aftermath or the reaping of transformation for a reawakening world. Moments awaiting the observing prediction to be found and shown.

Each day, she awoke early and expectantly for the near still and quiet of this time alone. She enjoyed this early morning and its abstract feeling of self-exclusion.

Outside, sitting on the sawed-off stump

near the extinguished, gray dust of the previous night's fire, she lit a cigarette as the early morning light gently coaxed back into hue the colors of day like a first deep exhalation of the sun freshly sweeping the gloom from the mountains with its bright breath.

There was similarity in the experiences of night everywhere as it occurred, whether in mountain forests or an urban alley and streets, change occurring and being spectated, sought out, found or coincided, existence occurring through the encounters and ensuing choices of its many intuited observers everywhere, wherever life can fit and in some small measure perceive, join and add to the ongoing, recurring natural exhibition.

There was a discovered resentment for the methods of its daily, evocative presentation. No perfectly attentive, emotional living being, a peculiarity of at least some small measure of human beings as Sela conceived it, could avoid the constant, obedient lure to ridiculously discard the balancing act of reality: a surrender not so much physical as weighted upon an unavoidable feeling, a feeling akin to scattered awakening minds suddenly stuck by the unsolvable nightmare of an invented, intended game-world, of being choiceless in a creation decided long before, of seeking and reaching realization at the precious cost of extraordinary souls splitting from the greater soul of its kind, and finding out late, within the solitude of each mind speechless with limited words to properly describe it, they must live or perish within the impure dangers such vulnerable aloneness of standpoint entails as the risks of exposed confidence.

The cost of realization, of the mutual detection of a living species with its world, was high. This was the time and the world Sela witnessed around her, a world inseparable from the countless unobserved millennia before and its shiftier blur still to come as an impending future: winning now the present sown by past impressions, of countless errors and mistakes, delusions and horrifying false paths, all perpetrated within a context of currently reflecting a past absorbed through mostly recklessness as it pertained to overpowering human successes. Blindsided by this success was the overwhelming veneration lost for the awe-filled world which came before it, a nature of wonder slowly evolving, as seen by Sela in the current state of the world, from resource of awe into faded imagination knotted with a looming future countenance of colorless, blurred horizons.

The question which revitalized within Sela's thoughts once again during these mornings, aroused by the fresh mountain environment surrounding her: *how is that my world?* This thought had always been a growing appreciation within her, even if she had to view back later to see it closely as a gnawing hindsight upon her original intentions of sincerity.

Recognition would often come later, but she learned to recall the patterns from experience as she sometimes did before they became anything large, aware, or believable within her as a truer involvement. She could imagine what occurred within her would occur within others too, and within humanity in the context of a social species, but this was not the reality she later learned occurred around her. Everyone lived in a singular state of belief, assimilating unique blends of talents, often connected to origins buried deep in an unrecognized, misshapen past.

It was a trying, dichotomous state the world had revealed of itself for her perspective, against the backdrop of an overwhelming nature endowed with living, connective presences now in the current state of the world, under her feet, and up high when she raised her head to mountains or stars as a fondling mutuality chased plainly and symmetrically.

Part of the cost of realization was the surge of recognition, the necessity of a continual, feeling experience, and the practical awarenesses of hindsight in her assembly of any moveable future involving her plausible belief in a path to properly follow as if an instinct like paved stones ahead of her.

The world was a difficult one to trustingly

traverse when an adverse, lingered past entangled itself too finely within the present. It forced an emergence of overcoming it as a survivalist strategy of mind and focus. To bear witness to the constraints of the world: the forces of an admirable universe influencing the becoming of alternatives, the comingle of revolt with popularity, hereditary prayer with artful new passions, and a disassociated past with a burning present.

She imagined herself freed of the many distractions of the city and her life there as she sat alone in the coolness of dawn trying to shed her unwanted, undifferentiating thoughts and a feeling jointly inspired by the stilled mornings during her earlier dawns in the mountains.

She wasn't totally freed, if such an idea was relevant in this world, but simply escaping to see a setting filled with a closer feeling of unfettered actions and choices. Though nothing and no one living was autonomous as Sela had learned to conceive of it through the interval of her experience and learning. She was attentive of the loose bounds between past, present and future in the experience of moments. Life as a moveable being was in its entirety restrained by emotions, bound to originating structures of mind, body, and reality in its manifolded representations.

Sela believed she was a measure of all she absorbed of the world around her, making it dangerous for her future to linger too many years inside the city's reflection, as the quiet of the early mornings in the mountains, with coffee and cigarette, the awakening glow of color, the fade of stars, and the quoteless recurrence of the close cheeps of small forest birds, bluntly reminded her.

During these few hours alone each morning, with only the increasing light as measure of her spent moments, it was the instances of excessive silence and stillness which reminded her of herself, her younger, childhood years spent near the ocean, a home enshrouded by the prevailing coastal forest, and the boisterous quiet she experienced, a quiet not without interfering waves of vibrations, for there were sounds, some hardly audible, others like the wind in the leaves, the awakening reprise of birds, the passing of a dragonfly; but a quiet of *feeling*, of mind, body and world beyond or merely between conflicts, away from events relatively occurring mostly everywhere else.

The sounds there and then in the early mountain mornings, concurrent with the rising sun, were the movements of silence playing with her thoughts of many equivalent past moments of quieted closeness near the ocean waters.

She felt freely separated from the rest of the world, for a short while, a few hours each morning, and embraced the rapport for the shortened stay she had to experience it at this time in her life.

She had to ask herself in solitude: "can you

live like this as habit, can you control this as sights to harvest instead of salt?"

~~

Like previous days during the trip, she let go of the past and future as best she could to enable her to enjoy the impending occurrences during the hike they had loosely planned the night before to take the next day. Sela knew it was her last day before heading back and the resonations of her future she had tried to avoid thinking about during her week there doused her early mood, supplanting her anticipation and attentions with a sense of woundedness.

She thought of this point in her life much like prior points forcing transition, growth, or self-evolution. She questioned again whether she had anything more to gain from the recently current life she'd been living. She needed to take further time to think through her "growing strategy" when she got back to the city as a symbolic cleansing for her path forward, before committing herself to planning anything else future-related in association.

She knew she couldn't properly move forward in her life until she overcame the impending test handed her, and one she was choiceless not to follow.

The only obligations she had at that stretch in her life were nonbinding future scenarios. She didn't have any real plan from there, just options, but she didn't need one right then.

For the time she was there, as best she could, she decided to leave all of *that* until after the mountains were viewably shrunken in her rearview mirror.

They had sifted through the trail maps of the area and picked the one they wanted to take for a hike. Starting early in the afternoon, the path began uphill. It wasn't long before they were walking through tall, old growth forest shaded with marked spurts of light jutting through the canopy to the lively, dense floor. The hard, worn path cut and meandered its way through the natural contour of the woods, firstly tall straight spruce and later locations populated with aspen.

Josh was subtle with his friendship the same as Sela, whether in the city or on a forest trail, and as a mannerism his usual demeanor appealed to her, allowing her to become closer with him than others she found among her prior and current, mostly transitory social relationships. She appreciated most his willingness to hold onto her as a personal connection for many years, creating a sense of relief in his presence with her, and preserving an unpresuming ease between them whenever they were together. He was rarely caught overlooking her in changing situations, groups or places, unless he was enacting a private romance with another woman finding in him something of what Sela saw but which didn't tempt her to intimate involvement for the sake of a rare prize she differently orientated upon as an enthusiastic delicacy to better savor.

Near the edge of a small bluish-teal colored lake, they stopped for a rest and vantage, sitting on the thick trunk of a fallen tree worn with use by years of prior visitors seeking out a similarly motivating vantage of nature, as if nature were a museum for the mind to sit, watch and recollect as the shifting landscape of a gifted, artistic craftsperson.

She spotted a hawk above the lake sketch a coiling mark across the sky and she hesitated at first to nudge Josh's attention to it, stealing the few moments for herself and the hawk without contrary urging. Josh didn't see it, looking behind him at the forest seeking a nearby spot to urinate as he got up and apologetically wandered off to do, she surmised.

It had been years since she had been of the habit of looking up and prudently aware of her environment, of knowing the sights she would routinely find as recompense for her attentions. For the bulk of her adult life, she studied and worked among others without similar memories of their own in private context; or else they all hid it as properly as she had learned to.

She had neglected her intuitions, forgotten her childhood insights she had originally, youthfully looked to find as the inspiring answer meant to be found elsewhere than where she was as an unspoiled mindset when she first ventured to this "*other world*" to her at the time, becoming habituated to its averting, downcast, timid stares of private spirits secreted voiceless behind mimicking personalities.

She had forgotten how often she had reminded herself as a teenager not to forget to keep her head up for the original amazement she felt and found then as the mutually imaginative stares of nature in reaction, spooked into action by her willful coincidence in looking.

She stared at the hawk's poised, effortless mastery of flow as its spiral gradually widened in her direction, with each twirl, a bit more of splitting redirection until the hawk, reoriented by briefly ageless moments, in agreement with a whispering smile roused to her face, hovered over the crests of the trees above her as she looked straight up at the white underside with wide, amber-speckled wings, and a twisted head pointed into her staring eyes in mutual, tangled wonderment for the tangible, fleetingly lasting moments of connection they felt together.

With refined, correcting tweaks of its feathers and muscle persuaded imbalances, the hawk wove its way slowly above and maneuvered around the peaks of the trees as she followed its path, standing, contorting her own body for best upward vantages and recoupling curtly lost perspectives of view, her vision focused beyond the gentle swaying of straight, whitish trunks bravely stretching upwards to the leafy ceiling shimmering in the wind against the lighted, bluish sky, each in unison seeking reciprocal sighted flashes of staring exclamations as she connected with the hawk's eyes reciprocal to the hawk seeking her eyes searching back in further adjustment to the speed and pattern of its rolling, weaving flight for no other cause than an equated, briefly rapt charm which would linger as a mutually emotive recollection beyond the meeker travels of time, and a cosmic sign for each to take forward as enduring depth for the other's distinctness.

This wasn't her first encounter with the connecting enchantment induced from reality through coinciding detection of higher-feeling predatory hunters and seekers of wayward enthrallments.

It wasn't the first time she was caught helpless like a fly in a web, entangling herself through the fleeting efforts inspiring a dual agreement of ownership through a merging, fixed stare wrought jointly with existence as a plaything of spirited amusements.

It lasted until the roving, intimate silence between them became disrupted by an unwitting

Josh reemerging from his respite further within the woods. Hearing his stomp, she wanted to whisper, "wait," but did not dare as the hawk suddenly, with one faint twist of its wings, while fixed in weakened momentum, hovered still upon the air, and the two sets of eyes waited for a few last moments before unavoidably breaking an interlocked contact for good and forever as the fates of lost lovers.

When she tried to further look, there was a faint, ephemeral blur, a symptom of her hope, and the hawk was gone.

She weakly motioned his attention up with her arm and pointing finger as Josh came along beside her, "a hawk, right up there, but I think it's gone now," she shared with him.

"I missed it. Should we wait?"

"Sadly, no point, I suppose it will find us before we leave if it wishes to see us again," she confided.

Continuing the trail, hopping by single leap over a fallen tree trunk crossing the path, Josh shamelessly voiced to her to take care while doing it. Though the intended reasonableness of his request seeped into her focus, its strangeness as a necessitated precaution lingered as an impending self-doubt.

His intention was a simple precaution, but

she hadn't predicted the need for extra care until he reminded her of what she had already been doing anyway. Releasing her sensitivity, she could see the caution was his in the way he sensibly, clumsily followed her lead in surpassing the natural impediments, uncovering another one of assortments of likeable imbalances between them and each other person in lively muddle of interpretations she needed to better overlook.

"These imbalances exist in all social interactions," she had uttered during a lazy conversation. He pointed out her poor handwriting on a scribbled note she had mistakenly left out, "making it challenging constructing the differing variations, but also our creativeness and passions which wouldn't be available without them," she had continued, reading the note herself after he passed it to her, and without recalling the exact context of the words, though they sounded like her and were written in her handwriting during another lateness of night consumed with raving wakefulness.

"There is the self-doubt which surfaces from what another might do wrong, which might be correct for them while not for you," she had scrawled as conjecture without context in the middle of a night.

Following the worn path at a pace upward through an olden thicket of brownish, crusted cedars, the trail began to loop and decline as relief from the straining upward hike to the mid-point as marked by a posted sign and viewable point of interest.

Her sojourn back within the proximity of nature, of facing its observant challenge in person, spotting its ageless signs and symbols, with a questioning mockery she couldn't help except see the same way as she had seen it in the past, as a fanciful, lusting awakening of herself found in involvement with its enthralled quests for playful deftness revealed to her as a suspicion of frolicking disobedience pushed upon her claim of identity, as a sense of loss, of a broken, misleading promise unfulfilled, or as a better maturity with a differently piercing glare.

During these experiences, she looked for the finer, bypassing details of the forest, its repeating patterns, shifting perspective of beliefs emanating as residual energies incredibly tuned to her senses and emotive inspirations, the varied textures, hues and changeable impressions uncovered with vividly devoted colors.

She explored the animated exhilarations on exposition for her scrutiny in the world, knowing each purposeful former image could be held for future illusory associations, and as benefit to herself. She wasn't certain how much of such retention most people seemed to possess secretively and selectively, but she had come to see the willingness of her memories to retain minute details and instances which stood out to her, even if not in the moment they occurred but as reflective reoccurrences when pertinent to the moment she was living in as new context, similar to a particular scent refreshing forgotten images of many years earlier in her experience by sensory association. Sela would find hidden images later as pristine subtexts, as private, vital orientations for her amusement and tracing insights too lately collected with regrets.

"I don't think there is much further left to go," Josh offered with a raised voice following behind her, "we've been heading down for quite a while," as she meandered around another sharp turn in the trail, obscuring him briefly from her angle of sight.

Around another bend soon after, the ground levelled under her step, opening into a field of interspersing arrangements of tall and trampled dried grasses and wisped, decolored wildflowers remaining from the year before under the melted snows, interrupted with sprouting weather-greyed tree trunks as haunted skeletal forms in the midst of temporal decay, a boggy land in the lapse of waste; "and only near the end," she considered as she stood waiting for Josh to catch up.

In the background, as an optic illusion of localized perspective, the smallish mountains rose larger as if peered at through a distorting lens.

Viewing the close mountains, she spotted a hawk again, or the same hawk, making her smile as she heard its single screech from its lofty, disillusioned height, ready to point it out to Josh for him to see.

But as Josh came along halting beside her, it wasn't at the hawk she directed his attention, and not with the carefree obviousness of a pointed index finger, instead evenly uttering in a focused tone, "stay calm, but there's a bear."

"Where?"

"Right there," she showed with a slight twist of her body until she was looking at it plainly, proudly standing in full, dark stature a short distance ahead alongside the path they were following, "but don't exactly look at it, or stare," she kept speaking evenly, "it's a mountain forest, black bears do live here."

Taking another twisting peek at the adult male bear as she knew from experience its shape and slightly runty size to be, she saw his head raise sniffing the air in their direction, then turning to look off, at Sela's leading cue, in another direction as their eyes broke contact after a lengthy briefness.

"Are you saying there could be more?" Josh calmly tested her.

"No, I doubt it, not right here, this one just

needs to find its own business, see us as just a coincidence here."

"Can we go back?"

"It's a long way."

Finally, overwhelmed with a frustrated lack of control, Josh raised his arms in the air, and firmly told the bear without rudeness or anger, "go on, get out of here, we have no interest to you."

The abruptness made Sela cautiously smile, as she watched the muscled, visibly male bear drop easily from its stance, then gingerly disappear as he sunk behind the leftover grasses and wildflowers; and she was sure in the moment she had heard a second, closer screech, as the hawk seconding Josh's imploration, from above and behind just as the bear relented.

Briefly the large dark mass reemerged as he crossed the path ahead with only a curt raise of his head and loud snuff at them before being gone from sight on the other side in the taller trees.

"Wow, that worked," she said.

"Think we can go?"

"Maybe we better give it a bit first. Then, it should be fine."

After a few minutes and many gulps of water, they continued the path. Sela walked ahead and Josh talked excitedly aloud of the thrill of the encountered bear as a promised strategy against reencountering it.

It turned out they were only a short walk to the end of the trail and a return to the parking space where they had earlier begun the hike.

"The experiences of some days stay with you and shape your future opinions of yourself. I guess this is one of those days," she told him later in the evening as they retold the encounter of the bear. "I'm glad we did the right thing. You were calm. Many people make the impulsive mistake of running or getting aggressive, instead of just being agreeable and confident," she proudly continued. "But don't go crazy with it!"

CHAPTER 2: MEANDERING PATH TO NOWHERE

The rocks softly grated beneath her footsteps following the leading, meandering route of the graveled path. The distinct scuffing was the same as during the day, but the quietness and less distracting lightness of night augmented the clarity as it spread and rung between the grasses, trees and scattered objects around the vicinity of the park's pathway. She listened to its soothing, singular clarity contrasted to the whiteness and noise of daytime. She tried slowing her pace to compensate for the disruption due her audible, scuffing awkwardness wandering solitary in the night. She listened for the recurrent, scuffling sound, but not the possible attention due its range disrupting her being a riven absence from her usual observed spectacle of awkward aesthetic attraction as a delicate, broken and untouched thing to the sighted sensitivities of this basely diverse reality she lived in.

She subsisted as an undetected flourishment in the cracked and fissured pathways of this worn urban world yet, as she was compelled by penalties to admit, differently to everyone else mostly comfily asleep in nightly cooccurrence. Sometimes, contrary to the observations of most as a rational, understandable justification, her impulses led her into doubtful happenstances, making of urbanity a dangerous place for her to live and brand a life styled without a personal context of placed identity to fully focus on as distraction from the seeping otherness of it as persuading obligation not naturally conducive to her attentively withheld, emotively poised state.

Yet what was life as guidance without perpetrating increased chances of incidences within the intimate parameters of her dominating cravings for risk? The true risk was in unearthing and originally challenging for feedback reality's countering exertions, to relax and trustingly show her signifying boundaries by imperiling and thereby finding her limitations as thresholds not yet surpassed, showing the "bounds of yourself as a capacity for willful, closely aware contest with the abundantly skillful outer world," she once wrote, "and to become better skilled in its nuanced, rebounding attractions."

The endlessly imminent menace of this nightmare-saturated world threatened the sincere ownership of her desires, through the context of so much crowdedness and her sympathies to its multifaceted impulses, raging desires, and bewildering beliefs. The empowerment of denials astounded her for the forcefulness of its penetrating obligation in all experiences she found, especially countered to her new perspective of urbanity against an alleged true, celestial value of meaning due her being unwittingly raised from an early age closer to nature.

In the city, there was overabundant source for significance to cling to, but none of it belonging to the representations of nature it sordidly insinuates through its imitating contortions, melding ideas with physicality as decadent icons for dominant human self-spiritualization.

It made her wonder, "what is it they found to reflect upon so devoutly in these symbols which I have missed out on and lack the sight to see and the emotion to feel with the same passionate association?"

The lacking was genuinely inside her as a fixed, intended restraint, and it was her improper inability to associate with the same permanence of deniability.

"These beliefs don't connect and hold with me the same as with them," she thought with quiet, composed explanation, for there was no one she directly confronted with her insinuations beyond her inner, endlessly roving emotive ruminations, as irrevocable, analog self-negotiation, and as surrogate for an intimate lacking in obtainable, faithful confidants as better guide. She had learned during her time here in this overarching world and its ensuing lack of meaningful discovery, she had only herself as guide to find the truer world.

She was shaped by all the multiplicity of presences reactive to her attuned understanding of herself as she had always finely found in her world, except for a recent lacking affinity to crowded individuality nudging her elsewhere for a better solace not being lived there. She had been spotted in marked contrast alike to the reading of spewed innards beyond the keen of her afire remedy to further absolve an urbanity with intimate descriptive ponderings of multiple fitting conclusions, and the manifold waves of other prodding, intersecting realities she roughly rode due the penalties of choices not belonging to her as will, choice, or preference, but by others rudely intruding upon her waves of reality as the residual ire of lessened, wasting determinations she had finally come to mostly absolve of her freshly selective attentions.

Whenever possible, she would exit and exclude herself for a time from those splashing, vibrant waves, seeking out a location, simply a hidden spot and its private moment, for stillness beyond the reach of the undercurrent, reeling forces disturbing the sprays into motion. The riskier the stillness of space and time she looked for and found, the finer the experience as a negligible, mimicking emotive poise for her soaring spirit to find proper winds to ride.

During those moments, it occurred to her, "the world would be so much easier without the discouragement of being alone. And reciprocally less impassioned as a motivated status into absence of appearance. So, a world without the threat of loneness would be an unchallenged world in which I never appeared to stand here seduced by the charm of its freeing release as a preference akin to a shared proportion with other animals and a rarity of humanity sketched by its seductive, entangled cues of choice," as she later wrote down for reason or fairness to herself as a recognizable, presentable occurrence.

She wanted to practice as an inner liveliness the exposed spectrum of her compelling dimensions as a living actuality dressed and mannered as a human woman by chance, for her willingness to believe, to calibrate the gifted skills between herself and the tangled, mystical reality of her genderless world, of the old, forgotten talents before the recognition of an alleged true giftedness as an atypical, uncontested peculiarity of her reality.

The ancient world was the same world then as now, except in its individuated beliefs, making within the confined textures of this world the mutuality of the old, altered world still seeking the same as it did anciently before, led through spanning temporal lengths and epochs of misled adventures with the melded excitements of only few staring, fixed contacts for rapport of its proven, isolated successes as coordinating reflection mirroring a spirituality in reality, a union not conjured but wrought through a differently associating plundering of reality, proven as her giftedness through the attuned countering of her intimate explorations of nature as reality's fixture for better challenge and the ethereal gems of withheld values and protections due her secret sightedness.

Her beliefs were wildly unutterable and verging on irrational abandonment without keeping herself in check through a trust in her revealing the full bounds of her privately caged captivity, to find the bewildering walls preventing her from looking beyond to further truths concealed by this veiled reality.

She wondered precisely where the concealment of reality from her senses began, showing itself as a caging shell through the transferring energy emitted from her sight into the obscurity of the shy universe as a surfacing, reticent camouflage hiding where she isn't supposed to peer, and the door deliberately locked to her imprisoned exit.

She would take long walks alone, thinly concealed by an otherwise mostly voiceless night. The uncertainty of others, just the distant sound of a hoot, a callous echo, or empty laugh would give her an injured pause or a fearless jolt to attention and replacement from her rambling, fresh recollections.

She could hear the hollowness in the sounds, the voided, genderless intentions in the inflected voices without eloquent confidence, and the fault of herself for hearing it as a challenge to a demanding delusion of practical comfort of mind. There was no getting away from the associations of reflected impressions absorbed by her intuiting, curious nature, and her sensory fierceness against waves of reverberating anticipations from which she unluckily sought releasing appeasement in the lateness of night.

Living in the city, she learned there is no certain future. She could plainly see the unsettled ending in sight for this abstracted world where so many were deserving of so much intentioned love reflected from so many others, with the illusion of commanding appearance, and a divergent sexuality as the lone quantifier of one's measuring spirituality. A world without authenticity, where each new stranger must be inspected for validity against the obviousness of deceit. A world of falseness, of false, worshipped things. "Where did this world come from?" she wrote. "It is already here on arrival."

It was preconstructed, predetermined as if without alternative, yet there it was in plain sight as the reality of a world to appear as a slithering, filthy thing of a concocted, mocking nature having predetermined an utter distain for existence, with humanity as the compassioned, lethal pill to a fitting end-game agony.

Too many years were spent since she arrived in the city, its exemplified world, as an overwhelmed stranger, as someone to have perceived and lived a brief truth, then being dramatically, violently cast away and self-exiled to the world of crowded experiences, of excessive, clowned personalities with confidently muffled stares. She didn't learn to appreciate recognizing the prior world as a unique value until she had lived long enough there inside its contrasting alternative, with its novelty worn and its assaulting ideologies perpetrated sufficiently against her the same as she had come to spot it in others around her as a silent vulnerability she learned to emotively assume as a privately seething, closing thunder.

Originally, she had come to the city as a student, a stranger, an outsider from a primitive world, because she had read the willing voices of worded humanity during her youth, a youthful sampling of books filling her with a desire for its experiences and higher learning she no longer wanted refreshing while she embraced the hopeless extent of her surrendering, impending retreat from it.

The world she found had turned on the world of history the same as it always had in the past, and the words she had read as a teenager were not meant to beckon but forewarn her against its venture, but one she was unable to discern without the direct experience of living it into an overshadowing new hindsight.

"The city is an open asylum. The patients lock themselves in at night."

Walking this pathway with Neal during a bright afternoon, he cleverly laughed, "and even doctors are patients."

"The old, punishing tricks of the asylum have been broadened to include the entire condition of society as the new raging discipline to aspire. The prior knowledge is not wasted."

"That's a way of looking at it," he had nearly silenced the conversation.

For Sela, the nausea came not from judging reality for its awkward naturalness of intending appearances, but in trying to understand it as simple truths to follow as guide and better fathoming of all its many plain, contorted exhibitions. "Somehow, we have to live with this world too," she clarified more to the sky and trees than to Neal, though it motivated him to nicely hold her hand as they further walked.

~~

In the lateness of night, she had left him

asleep in her bed and snuck out quietly locking the apartment door behind her. She had been prone beside him for hours staring at the barely lit darkness, unable to sleep before sating her itch to rove as private deal for a return to tiredness upon her arrival back, ready to dispel her insomniac loop, to allow the air to clear the reoccurring, contrasting moods torrenting upon her thoughts.

"The disenchantment of impending death inspires an enthusiasm for a disowning, celebratory kind of rejection of the olden world in favor of a newer, reinterpreted and kinder world for such newfound, indelicate awe to fittingly trace as replacement of worn, historic journeying," she had slowly recounted.

Neal didn't reply, not knowing exactly what she was talking about, which the same as prior instances made her indelicately smirk to herself as a thing regretfully found once again in the world as a slanderous, dejecting routine without alertness. He didn't always know how to reply, as she could tell by his silences, and she didn't question it due its resurfacing appearance in past related encounters with others, within its scope as a private, cooccurring association, which gave her an answer of him in association with her like all the rest as a belief to follow with less seriousness.

She had nothing more to add to the one-sided conversation, while his gaining distance and unfocused attentions assured her it was permit-table to continue a relationship with him since the bond between them was weakly tolerable in mutual favor of a physically connective one less emotionally risky for the inevitable, predictable loss of a merely conceived, acted-upon habit alongside the reciprocal "expectation of nothing more between us," the same as between herself and anyone else as a better personal integrity to live by.

They walked under the fresh sun while she watched the bypassing wet grasses and sidestepped clear puddles coordinating her movements along the pathway. A magpie kept peeping from the trees, hidden behind the quivering leaves, pricking at her narrowed focus as a hinting interruption keeping her within the moment and giving the moment its sole, lighted flicker different than a counting anticipation.

Sometimes, she forgot others didn't really see or correlate to see her contrast as an unaffected person, though she predictably knew as it pertained to Neal her words weren't much within his range of interest in her since they lacked the carnality of the physical body as enticement. In this way, she could wildly opinionate, opening herself up with him knowing whatever she said didn't much matter one way or the other, with the result being comfortably predictable without deviation for its leastness to his sense of meaning. There was a kind sense of well-being in this aimless, precluding conversation marked as relationship between them.

"It's comforting to think the universe goes back farther than is reachable by our emotional thoughts, mathematics, theories of origin and our fringed imagination," she abruptly countered the lingering silence.

As he often did when he meant to reply to her attempts at conversing with him while he didn't nicely listen or wish to pursue her words with further interest, he said, "I never much thought of it that way before," adding the kindly false encouragement with the enthusiasm of a fixed smile and a brief elevation of his stare, revealing expectantly again his contented disinterest in her other than bodily by his slight effort at connection contrary to her uniquely baited words cued to him, forging her irresistible attraction to him as a perfect fit for the time.

The more obscure she playfully, astutely lured his inattention of her, the closest to herself she convincingly spoke aloud, the more she expectantly nudged his common, impassively quieting retorts as his requirement of turn.

It wasn't disappointing to her, though it was reassuring to know a lack of emotional seriousness was shared between them, allowing her to continue a physical attachment without spending much of her emotive energy crazily factoring the many skewing undertones normalized by related associations within the world of urbanity she had striven through for the means to a successful overcoming of it.

She intended gathering the values of its insights, purposes, and then discarding it, as she will inevitably with Neal if he doesn't before her, with no further use for it as furthering excitement for her private emotional sensitivities linked to the actions and encounters of the world shaped around her as descriptive, illusory experiences destined to the fusing fates of meanings lost or found through a whispered, private exposure to a reality teasing her to prove an opined individuality as either right or wrong, and as properly due for an impending and clouded future version of Sela to find out somewhere else.

Also, he kept her from sleeping alone on occasional nights as a juxtapose to her usual aloneness, though just as often she could do without him there in the morning when she awoke with a tinge of regret over her continuing weakness at properly navigating the subtly dreaded intimidations of aloneness.

The recent encounter with the bear had stirred her memories, confounding any fresh ideas she had of herself being capable of moving willingly into the future without contending with the past in its obvious, troubled manifestation upon her psyche, and a potential danger to others, as an unfinished contest she had to contend.

She had lost focus of herself, something newly discovered to be her earlier lucky adornment of her unbeknownst personality blended into a comingling of emotions not belonging to her, confusing what was hers as ownership and what belonged to others as fitting source of touch, acting upon her as broken barriers or shrunken boundaries closing in with claustrophobic abandon. She had long begun to specify a palpable separateness between herself and others, without searching for it but as a simple emergence from her prior experiences into a current naturalness of new, maneuverable choices.

The trait she had found instinctive in the world, and which truly caused her moveable reactions of mind, was the awareness of so many people living out of control, without the modesty of integrity as self-mastery or inner connectedness with primal awarenesses.

Instead, she was subdued by populated solutions of physical and psychical constrictions with nowhere to truly soar in a place she was meant to flourish, thrive, and master as a living entity and emergence into the world.

"Through differing senses, some individuals should experience less separation between identity of self and environment, to naturally assume a private closeness with existence rather than the counter mainstream of the spectrum consumed with over-assumption of self as an intimately over-sensory detachment from environment. Such differences of sensory associations with reality, such ranges or frequencies of perceptual skills in bodily instincts pulse through the multifaceted predatory designs of nature the same as in the telling, desperate and reactionary designs of all prey," she had written a few nights before and then earlier in the night reread it with the same sense of detachment between herself and her written words as a context of reality.

In general, she discovered other people didn't seem to delve far into things, as a convenience of conscience, with less awareness equating to less culpability, poisoned on fears of any alternatives, contending there were no faults to be had in subscribing in common to one assortment of many assortments of ancient, measured beliefs as excuse of willpower enough for the absolving of answerability.

Self-infliction and rage should be commonplace after so many ages punishing against retribution as an innate, psyched reaction. She sought the signs of its emotional state as witnessing victim through the daily reoccurrences of her furthering experiences.

Living in the city, she reviled the detection of herself relenting to being passively intimidated by the intended looks in multitude, and not so much at her as also all around her in prismed directions from multiple locations, swept up with the whirlwinds of other strange unknown entanglements, coercing her repeating thoughts to quietly despair her cowardly unwillingness to leave the city for what it tendered in return as impending futurity. She was panicked by either choice as mutually approachable or escapable to her benefit.

She had avoided and run from the challenge due her own restricting reserve, with her inhibition to go back and continue within a world she didn't much know or fully appreciate but had found to be existing within this reality as a deviating force, its disassociations permeating all encounters, and spread like a silent, unchecked contagion. Still, she needed the city experience, its learning and alluring, penetrating depths of fathoming contrary to her usual understated personality, furthering in retrospect an infectious transition from a natural reality she had experienced as a nightmarish sight to others and confident encouragement for herself to quietly experience, an unlit shadow mimicking her actions as an astute chaperon, befriended by her own memories as by a roving ghostly spirit haunting her past self as careful companion seeking the clues to her strange reality vicariously through Sela's experiences as the sole source for meaning.

"The waving spirit of never-ending death and rebirth," she heavily empathized in script, "can such a brave vow of silence be trusted held eternally captive to the first strings of life?"

There was no one to talk with genuinely about what would require utter trust to tell within the confines of the current world, giving her the self-impression of being an outcast to her kind, tribeless within a species where living moments had become replaced by ticking, counting seconds measured by the spinning of sticks.

She spoke indirectly of herself to others without much disclosure of past or future details, without much belief in others seeing her proper context of experience in her beautifully reflected peculiarity.

She could see what seemed an old world then existing later in pocketed locales and secluded findings, during private moments stolen from the countless milieus of chanting togetherness as meditative intimacy through her absence of true involvement amongst gatherings of people, though she preferred at times the physical closeness of focused, directed crowds and privately passioned agreements acting in unison. Briefly at times, she enjoyed seeing the closeness in the city through the changing tones of strangers as an empathic, blissed separation from herself.

~~

"What is that worth to study? Philosophy? Good luck making a living with a degree in *that* as a major," directly associating the value of learning to material output, though he was a stranger at a party, and she knew strangers could be prone to expound such disregards as advice to her or any other unsuspecting listener.

"Well, it can teach you to think, for whatever that's worth in this world as an advantage, which could be considered just about everything," she replied. Often, such commonplace negations of meaning had to be defended against an otherwise emptiness of conviction prevalent in others even during her four years at university among the higher educated within the walled commoditization of learning.

More simply, philosophy as a pursuit gave her the encouragement to speak for herself, to wildly, creatively elucidate with lessened discomfort when the opportunity was presented within the social entanglement, though it wasn't usually amply present as a normalcy of interactive conversation due to the tendency for its potent, aphoristic origins to shatter into intense dispersions when confronted by the array of reality with its real, intended and opined associations of intense playfulness inevitability turned into the ploys of countless unseen redemptions in reluctant need of urgent sating.

It was an excuse to be artful or fancy without appearing unusual of interests and questionable as quest of mindful detection of the world as an actual pursuit of existence in all its colored vigor of revelation. This was not something she could much explain candidly to another person without the inexhaustible, creative artistry of philosophy as a trait of her persona in which to quietly sate the fearful enchantments of thoughts and playful, inventive ideas as a revolting, rousing impression upon others.

Sela acted and spoke under the cover of philosophy's painted, clownish face, baggily costumed with amusing, floppy high heels.

She was putting the effort into making an attempt at personal collectiveness with others she chanced to find the experience of contact during her years of education and employment, like a great artist in spirit with the creative ambitions but without the talent to create great works of art for others to scrutinize and measure for truer value as an identity within the world of gambling talents, without the returnable channel for uttering a celebrated communication, attempting to find a middle ground within this urban, populated world, a commonness on which to tread like the stones of a beach, near the merging threshold of water, land and air in full and abundantly fruitful, lighted spectacle; but this was a squalid, urban ground on which to tread, freed of philosophical pangs and the moral dilemmas of unobserved karmic events unevenly twisting the contorted values of reality from which it originally sprung with the suspicious quietude of first wonders long ago.

"This is a dangerous place," she whispered alone one night, "a pressing intensity of daring experience from which to reciprocally challenge and mutually exclude."

She felt as "the future vision of an ancient wanderer's realer mystical journey. I'm an omen in an ancient vision predicting a time not yet arrived!"

Going there, studying, gaining her degrees, working and living all these years in urbanity with its tolerant stomach for otherwise inedible ideas, she had found a disciplined fury punishing her while not belonging to her, and not belonging to anyone in isolation but as a communal, doubtful rage disguised with threats, reaching prides and impaled backbones.

She could not figure out her crime as precisely as she ached for its investigative solution. She had come to personify the same unsolvable crime they had all committed while pleading a raging innocence with silent ignorance.

"Generations born on strict, coexisting rebellion and adherence in perpetual conflict over rightness. A history of struggle and revolutions for this endgame to occur," she had written in a notebook, "and with such tempered passivity to fade back into timeless infinity. The struggle was never fittingly just, even, or worthy as an appropriate response to a brief, mistaken, cosmic awakening from eternity, the rapid, forgotten dream of a venerably slumbered universe."

~~

Being with another person as a commitment, as an attempt at meaningful, freeing rapport within the repelling margins of urban reality, beyond the role of integrity as a common, lurking absence whether through the attachment of another or the self-attachment of being alone, she sensitized too acutely the separateness of every endeavoring affection to own her.

She begrudgingly had to admit of herself, as a caution to heed in the safeguarding of memories to keep as latent, impending penalties for her future to better grasp, knowing, "the mind is trained by its memories," and the natural world guided by voiceless, karmic reckoning equally practical as blissful, helpful fulfillment too.

She found over the years of private, internalized studies in relationships occurring despite a previously predicted faithful adherence, and the unsolicited, unearned fallouts of its callous gameplaying, that she was not capably adapted to traditional ideas of associated merger. She was made vulnerable by her acute sensitivity to its consequences and the lengthy depths of her self-punishments; before recognizing the associating patterns requested by sufficient experiences of contended, reoccurring interruptions of her emotional state trackable to the distrusting maneuvers of others as a willful, uncontested force habitually acting against her well-being in favor of trait-minimalizing group dynamics.

It was a crucial step for her to accept the evenness of not adhering to traditional ideas not her own to avow, reached from the labyrinth library of past solutions no longer relevant to her while still being guarded at its fitting vulnerability in others as a heeding awareness of pervading mistrust in the benefits of experience from a world prevalent with misplaced honors, as a world of unpracticed heroes and untrained, defanged and preyed-upon predators tamed in open cages.

Not that she couldn't live up to such a true and worthy devotion as "aloneness," written by itself out of context on a scrap of paper, or as an endeavor or way of life, she simply couldn't think it any longer truly possible in a world which tested *aloneness* for the measure of its depths as insights, prodding it tethered into the open as an exhibition of a reality observing it, poking its hungered artistry with sticks and slaying it with stones.

At least for Sela, the raging interpretation of solitude was an earnest hunt to disavow as if it never truly deserved its contorted misplacement "as a role and rule of punishment by loudly other believers intended to silence its intimidating pains upon the souls of the voiced," as she once wrote for no one else to read.

Being partnered with another person wasn't an easy thing, and she often made it "harder than it had to be," as she recurrently heard from anyone to get that close until she laughingly screamed at another happing absence while sliding into the seductive burden of a different other's willing, excited embrace after finding her eagerly gazing in reply. It was easy and less a distraction as a style of life, for there were always a plentiful supply of other awaiting embraces in the city, and different only in suckled convenience to the less opportune remoteness of her upbringing as choice.

She found as a sole source for such true or hearted devotions occurring within the confined pages of authored imaginings where such value shone bright as an easy, pure predicament of an attuned reality happening between powerful protagonists and the coinciding, hidden creation energizing actions as the flow of words printed for her attentive, practicing imagination to absorb in hidden light.

An impossible commitment had to be a necessity for her from someone else, and she no longer believed it could be a shining emblem of chance after succeeding the reoccurring, draining aftermaths on her bodily sanities as too high a cost to risk for the benefits given as the loss or betrayal of her easy devotions at the wily impulses of less sincere others.

Inevitably, her past devotions were wrought with an evolving separation between herself and the charms of urban reality, much as with sipping snake venoms as a building impunity to the tease of further biting provocations, and a fuller, truer balancing between her body and the urban scape swarming her. She believed her time in urbanity to be a seeking, unbiased compromise to a layered, complexing discipline she meant to overcome for its illusory, creeping influence upon the impending versions of usable certainty. She lived here during these years as a defense for her later self, and the many strangers of herself she had yet to meet while determined later through her earlier choices for herself then.

She sympathized with the girl and younger woman she was before she learned to toughen her expectant staring and cling to a purer reality beyond caricatures drawn from the ideas of the past, a new world of open devotions to embrace and fling asunder as a practicing lifestyle, as a pronounced assumption of her formulating urban personality actively freed of its seductions enacted through the loose threads of entangled social involvements. More often, she watched herself simply casting down or disinterestedly away as an appropriately missing participation she couldn't resist adhering to as a continually renewing self-discipline to further uphold.

"Being part of reality, it's there to see if people want to look and find it, just nobody believes enough to look. It's something that could be shared, a unifying force of incorporeal attraction between all, but there isn't sufficient belief of similar kind to share it merely with one individual possessed of its mindset, and instead shunned as its outcast," she had told herself rather than abuse into existence the words through the callous rumbles of her voice. It was best kept silent, for the thought didn't matter or act as leap into action so long as she controlled it instead as a force of restraint, evolved through its peripheral encounters alike to its inner silences as unending, associating rapport.

This world was not the real world, but one to be assumed as supreme within the idea of itself as the utter importance of the universe. A world truly dishonored and to which she had become an unwitting accomplice. "There is no truth here, what could that mean?" she wrote somewhere on a restaurant napkin, crumbled it up and dropped it dabbed in the smeared whitish film of her emptied soup bowl opined under the weight of the spoon.

She wondered on her obligation to this place, or to her species in the prolonged current condition it had adopted as a reality for itself to live up to. She became victimized by the urban world through the mere fact of becoming its witness and through an inexperienced closeness to its multitude of strangers meant for appeasing befriending without attempted fathoming, making of Sela a stranger and outsider loitering among the entwining world of friendships belonging to others for her to see and minimally partake.

Sela believed herself to be wary for her reproachable contentions, as such ideas tended to distend beyond an original shell of intentions into new polluted realms of defeat and how that defeat, which occurred as unperturbed sparks ignited by the forgotten origins in history, had its sightedness cast upon an all-encompassing endgame of downfall for the world she observed with a dithering realness of vision, perhaps obvious through an abrupt, inhibiting contrast against the secluded life of her youth encroached within a natural sanctuary mostly far removed from the conception of urbanity as an experience of a different style of belonging.

People she met were too emotionally unpredictable to not be rightfully cautious and wary afforded to a lacking in deep awarenesses, each floating the surfaces with perilous, suspicious, watery depths below and endless, cheerful skies above.

Though, as she had learned, she rarely experienced fear, not due to a sheltered lack of need for its pricking, but as a felt, practiced absence.

In the city, no one ever mentioned nature without there being a human attached relationship of context. It wasn't ever an approachable topic of conversation without a dangling human background for ownership to fathom, segregated into proportioned, conveniently charitable, human-sized lots of appropriately appraised analysis to properly opinionate of the peculiar world of nature spotted here and there throughout the course of eons of generations; and consensually too afraid to look and see.

~~

Instead, this was a weighted world affirmed by the oscillating pendulums of sexual dominance and spiritual fantasies as the motivating backdrop for themed carryings-on. Instead, a world fabricated without focus, with inhabitants unable to create new, original concentrations, attracted to the raising of downcast milieus for betterment and the permeating humiliation of buried, self-inflicted defiance like the cutting mutilations of past prides.

The swiftness with which atmospheres could abruptly change as an unchecked routine, from shifting induced states to shifting induced states, the intoxicated energies between individuals and among groups, where a newfound bliss can just as readily become an instantly transformed antipathy of equal energy as a balancing counterweight, so that the achieving of bliss, if partaken, becomes a locally confined cosmic debt.

Her moods, the same as everyone else, were persuaded by the altering moods of all the others surrounding her, creating unowned, clownish performances making her reciprocally spectacle and onlooker of herself as the one acting her role, bound locally together as a unifying force of mutual, tempered encouragement accorded the waves of mimicked reality, a different sort of ruled natural order against the background of the old natural world misrepresented as "an ancient, impending fossilized wasteland for human misconduct to make use as a proper new order is instilled for better consumption harvesting the receding multiplicity of a prior evolutionary world's success igniting its inevitable de-evolutionary fate," she despised herself for fathoming and writing of an approaching, slouching beast of a reality rather than the poetry of trees.

She had questioned and seen the expounding of assorted beliefs in people, and when confronted with a challenge of integrity, of broader elucidation, the system quickly decayed and scattered into utter, dusting disownment mimicking the branding confusedness of a challenged, deeply held disbelief.

Honesty was at issue in this world, conflicted and battled over a seeming eternity as a weakened sentiment to privately care for and hide if felt as a backwardly natural, sole response to the world, as if darkness looked for light and cold sought heat; compared to the benefits afforded the use of simple falsehood as a predatory trait she had been too inexperienced to avoid falling prey.

"For most successful individuals, karma doesn't always seem to be paying attention, or else it is building its violent pressure for an impending, forceful future within which to voice more properly its tangled, screaming retort, a volcano with pressure blocked deep inside crafting an impressively explosive escape which results in a changed world. There is a base state of illusional being people tend to find highly popular and real as a calming haven for attention," she broodily wrote on a torn piece of paper, reread it and dropped it in a desk drawer with many others connecting an echoing current pattern with her personal past within the repeatedly restricting space of her apartment and her conjecturing routine of writable mental objects as assorted artistic sketches for her later, reminding use: as many thin rubber bands tightly wrapping her fingers and toes.

Her constantly checked emotions had inevitably become disjointed and untangled from the fabric of any solid inkling of herself among all the sharing crowds, like a tattered, unlivable life after being figuratively torn to shreds, so that she no longer sensed her feelings or wanted desires to be purely of her possession, yet they lingered recurrently inside her body as a numbing omission, as the frayed unravelling threads of her former self-confidence, as the thing she mostly always knew before as an obvious portrayal of the current world she lived in without its valued privilege as possessive disbelief of another reality behind and alongside it, a reality she experienced to be actual elsewhere as a prior sounding still resonating across millennia, of an attaching, temporally enacting vigor meant for the renewal of perpetual reoccurrence.

Sometimes, exhausted by abstracting all the daily multitude sanctioned in obvious collaboration, she later noticed herself being wrong in her interpretations of an emotional or mindful state she thought she perceived in the atmosphere of the world, punishing her with humiliating hindsight at her wary, indiscrete imaginings. She believed a sight, or a hastened chime of emotion, always belonged to her and pertained to her as context, while it was commonly a belief from another she misconstrued as a reflection meant for her. She couldn't support with consistency all that which related to her and which to others within the moments, torturing her with personal regrets and inhibiting her later, intimate attempts at relationships.

The hardship was in her sightedness, in her

past experiences of unbeknownst openings, her regretful fears, tears and trialing weaknesses, leading her to need to be capable, seemingly with will, to not see through volumes of other experiences not belonging to her, to separate through an attentive filtering of herself from her emotively influencing environment's tendencies upon her body's senses, forcing her to try to ignore and turn away from the less original aspects, to downcast her eyes as a daily, meditative reprieve and self-discipline through the lens of these awarenesses.

This disparity between herself and others seemed to exist in most social exchanges whereby only the momentary fulfillment was seen, and she found herself helplessly pulled into its submerging riptides the same as all the rest without taking culpability for her reoccurring inhibitions and poor swimming skills.

It became that she couldn't trust in herself, instead becoming suspicious of her thoughts, experiences, emotions as no longer belonging to her in ownership, instead becoming the absorbed, imitating reflection of others she met and accidentally shared together no different than the light bouncing and being absorbed among and between all the stuffs of a moveable world.

This world had taught her to pay careful heed to her imagination sparking excitations of events and visions of people romanticized contrary to a firmer, wily reality challenging her to see as heed its truer side.

"There is no correct path in this world of countless conflicting indecisions, each constantly interjecting with all the other, contrary, staring perspectives justifying the denials of awareness for opportune social, politicized and admirable self-advantages conjured from the prismed distrusts of mutual complicity.

"I can't conceive, as dream or nightmare, how this world belongs to me. I don't believe in it as success, yet here I am compelled to belong and made to witness its beliefs with open eyes," she later worded to her journal as if an apologetic excuse for her injured escape.

Later as an emerging adult, within the context of opposing ethers of comprehension, she came to better accept the tints of strangeness inundating the range of her experiences from her intimate and superficial origin with the bursting appreciation of a stranger's ownership, a difference of perceptive absorptions of reality's surging, manifold textures. She came to view these aspects as strange, frightful symptoms of her difference. The fright only occurred after living away for so long, as a pang of regret at a former, lost self-identity and a humiliation of faith.

This world practiced its recurring moments, scaling the spectrum heights of connotated truths without any true belief beyond the dominating of self-wills, fixated by its charms, spellbound and intoxicated by the many tonics it approved for humankind as a choice of reality for each to affirm; while firmly held and violently defended, a world sprinkled with individuated faiths. Within this world, on occasion and by the mere accident of a wildly ranging volume of coinciding experiences, an individual happens to unwittingly chance upon a genuine penetration of reality into a quality of the universe which might closely imitate the genuine compulsion towards truth capable of its species in latency; an impending, immediate truth with no pressing value other than its keened consideration as a glimpsed wisp of a wordless, floating solitude soon faded and lost until freshly manifesting in a different context of visualizing isolation somewhere or somewhen else.

On rarer occasions, a willful individual will discern the otherwise indiscernible, as the mimicking embodiment of nature's discovery of reaching solutions birthed from absence and follow it after fruition as a secret practice of quiet attainment otherwise ignored by the preoccupied multitude of a species, owner of a suspect sightedness newly claimed as student to the mentorship of an exotic ability entwining reality.

It was hard to imagine a whole lifetime in this urban environment, among the surrogates of nature all the time, occurring and practicing with them a privileged life in style. A buildup of such a naturally conical mindset, confused by years of living a battlefield of manifold, conflicting self-dramas contending for an optimized renouncement of anything actual other than the randomized crowing of personalities discerned as juxtapose to the wordless cawing of a realer world.

No one she came upon in the city knew of a difference other than the alternative they assumed and built upon as a true origin of birthright. They had no belief in existence or forces of nature, and the things they did believe made no lasting sense except as the comforts of denial, and a relaxed, instinctive attachment with it; rather than accepting it as a challenge in mocking lightness to confidence melded to the segregation of temporal moments as the excuse for the trickery of continued agreement of a life coursing the heftier risks of lethality following alternative, ungrouped choices.

Sela was harmonized by a different agreement with the instincts of reality, and a loftier emblem of nature hinted to her from her undeniable sensory associations of a cooccurring eventful world as the moveable object of her observations of it, as if brought into reality by her singular observation of it, like a particle stilled by the retelling proof of light spotting its physicality.

In situations while interactive with other people, she discovered she usually applied the unspoken question "*why?*" to her later and in the moment introspections, inhibiting her ability to proceed in reoccurring social panoramas without the care of an answer she never finds, while endlessly refreshing new "*why's?*" and "*what's?*" and "*how's*" continually surfaced in the roving moments not slowed alongside her inhibitions the same as in everyone else, occurring over spans of encounters and ranges of interactions forcing her to exist as if dragging in time, slowed by the streaming pull of change occurring and attracting her perceptions within and behind the experiences of the world around her, while circularly seeking out her own involvement without an immediate answer, symbiotic to reality's challenging actions encouraging her further vigilant, questioning deliberations promised for her worldly attentions to intimately prey upon her self-image as "an existing, shaped identity out of context with my world."

In this way, the gameness of reality might consume her, forcing her to inevitably recognize herself and settle her raging rapport with the contrary new world of reality she hadn't been trained for as a child. She'd been raised a child meant to be excluded from the urban world, or to be its victim upon her impending arrival without foresight of her needs once there. Unbeknownst and unprepared, given her circumstances, she had once ventured out until now she stood flattered and numb, her past impressions riddled by its harsher memories as a broken, pock-marked landscape to freely navigate into her future.

Her moods and emotions were no longer her own to be considered, being recurrently distorted by the ravaging reflections of others around her, in the moods of their glimpses, the faint echo of intelligibility as grandness, of confidence in a binding solution meant as multifaceted, manifesting strategies of a confounding dominance. She was no longer in full possession of herself the same as everyone else appeared to be. Emotional entanglement spread like thrashing waves through the populace, and she was caught treading such virulent depths, pushed and pulled in many directions by the overwhelming violence of it focused within herself as a newly reinforced context of rebellious, carefully treading awarenesses.

The initial quality she had believed to be a difficulty and deficiency of nature created as anomaly within herself had shifted as an opinionated self-diagnosis over time, while living there, to be a sharp difference between herself and her inventive surroundings, complete with the many distinctly shaped faces assumed for the benefit of its many inhabitants; but "it means nothing to me," as she pulled her sleepless self from her bed to write in her journal one night without further elucidatory context, then went back to bed and finally to sleep with expectation of another renewed morning to come, finally freed of the incessant patterns storming around in her thoughts, her fresh emotions ready to be reassumed once again as a new day awoken in kindness to her sensitivities of it.

CHAPTER 3: DEAD-END PLATFORM

"Have you never noticed," she said to Rey during her fourth year at university, in reply to his heartfelt, early-warning admission he had deep feelings for her after a few months of relationship, "everyone uses love here as an unsheathed weapon? It's a dangerous scuffle to get involved with, and I wouldn't recommend it for you, as I don't for myself. I don't just mean with me. I learned that my first year."

It was a bit harsh of her as she recalled the conversation as an association later in a different context valid to maturity, though she was correct not to relent, to know the common carelessness of words used conveniently in the moment without the clever command of permanence, and she bravely stood firm in her impassioned disinterest, disavowing the sympathetic cowardice of avoiding a presented moment with the preferred choice to evade with precious words of false consolation masquerading as a confidence of future chance.

She continued her cutting words with callous, blood-scenting disregard, "in fact, I can prove it to you it isn't really genuine affection you have for me. It's important to feel love and warmth at an early age, as you likely did by your sensitive words, even though it will inevitably become lifelong struggles, capitulations, and conflicts as the adult tries to simulate what the child in you found readily available but no longer applicable to the genuine, imitating world of adults, except as the advance of vulnerability due to its growing absence as a reachable truth in your life. You are fixating that vulnerability on me. It's normal, we all do it," her voice began to ting with excitement. With a few calming breaths, she paused to slow down her mood as she was accustomed to do when requested by her challenged body's spotted excitement rushing her words to keep up with her thoughts.

"Are you psychoanalyzing my emotions towards you? It sounds like you're philosophizing my expression of feeling," he challenged her during vulnerable, reflective moments urging Sela's self-recognition, of moments stilled to a single moment by her private withdrawal from time while it continued for him by the same pace as before.

"No, we're just talking, I'm explaining, you were open with me, I recognize the trust you give me, and I want to be open with you too, and return the trust. It's just how I talk. I really can't help it. I thought you might have noticed by now," as she twisted and poked the end of his nose with her finger to recoup an active confidence; then she became focused upon the discomforting, lacking familiarity in her dismissive gesture completely unlike her.

The self-confidence formerly held for this unbiased relationship was shattering and she was a mere spectator of its polite dissolution. A bond was breaking loose into new likelihoods of impending, diverging paths she had chosen not to follow in her past many times as the unavoidable escapades of emotional dramas entangling lives, the ensnarement of a broken perfection once prescribed for herself as inclusion, but such dramas were illusory, transitory and now reserved solely for others as Sela learned to keep her familiarities and any residual expectations in check as the wary self-preservation of her psyche's wellbeing.

"It should be okay that I expressed my feelings, we have emotions, it doesn't have to be equally reciprocated. I think I just felt the need to say it, so you would know," he justified.

"Don't we become clumsy when we talk about sharing our feelings. I always find it awkward. Don't you? Shouldn't everybody?" She continued to make the effort as the current sanctuary faded before her senses with disenchanting predictability of resulting emotional trials and its loosening of controls.

She was a natural masochist when it came

to maneuvering through the entreating, callous emotional spectrum of relationships, thriving on the welcoming negativity of excitements as predicted self-allure newly staged with pertinent drama for each new relationship.

She continued, twisting her nakedness to the side beneath the blankets to see him directly again, "I think most interactions and relationships in life are mainly compiled of strategies, rooted in nature's games, to which we, as individuals, have assumed as our styles of life too, as an idea of an imitation of nature, for lacking better skills or imaginations."

"You're reasoning my emotions," he gleaned from her words.

But to her it was "simply the way I talk, and you maybe need to listen better. Our emotions should be critiqued. People often spread affection without the skill of listening to know if the feeling is real and deserved, or to be bothered with the care to listen. In my case, I have to say it shouldn't be *this* real."

"Couldn't it be? I'm simply making an expression of a feeling now, not predicting the future."

There had been many others through her years in the city she saw as friends she often later avoided as respect for her relatable impossibilities due the world of interacting social promises. It was a world she couldn't properly track in the moment without an ability or outlet to better explain and be properly heard, with no one to give proper circumstance contrary to her gracious actions to avoid any seriousness with her relationships as much as people can be taken seriously in a frivolous world.

"Perhaps it has been said before, or you have not felt it yet as truth, but hate is indistinguishable from love," she coldly iterated, as in fact she was disappointed by the night's turn of events, for she had liked him more than most other short-lived friendships she brought into and out of her life, with the same deviation from normalcy she aspired as a balance with both strangers and friends alike. She had, in her own, odd, indecipherable way tried to be honest and show integrity as an expression of her uncertain affection for him due to him simply being "one of everyone, including me."

Her unbending honesty usually tended to play out badly in a fantastic environment of leading actors playing roles sharing the same worldly stage, further encouraging her social awkwardness as the avoidance of her guilt at perpetually seeing a permeating dishonesty surrounding her as trustworthy of keeping merely *unfelt* emotional attachments. This condition of identity encouraged her as an enhanced, undeserving durability upon her recollections of loss while becoming too distractive an overlapping hindrance upon her daily, emotional psyche, affording depressed states she had no interest in further having to tend to as private debt in her ongoing life, forcing a rebelliousness against herself realized as criminal rather than as victim.

Sela had no interest in allowing another protagonist to exhaust her within his newly imposed, active role, rather than the gathered identity she played as leading relationship within a shared performance all her own.

She couldn't simply shun all contact, even if it was difficult to take each new contact seriously beyond the allayed moments in the comfort of a predefined, biased trust hard to find outside her solitude, usually better as a noncommittal, emotionally played trust without risk of further punishments, especially since she detested being stung and long strung out on the culpable feelings of her prior enactments. "By what peculiar twist of fateful entanglement do I end up the perpetrator in these outcoming events?"

With each new break-up, she questioned the value she represented as a precast, understating role among entities of everyday transaction. She couldn't attach belonging or true ownership to these transitionary relationships she kept close as a best adaptable choice for her private appeasement other than as the heartfelt entreaties of some of her unannounced, unwitting emotional victims due her need for experiences to foster her future self, though she couldn't perceive such things as victor and loser, as subjugation and domination, nor as cold, dirty games being playing with and across lives.

Her capped seriousness among people was justly deniable given her past involvements as indelible memories coaxing her new intentions as a juxtaposition during the present of her intimately occurring events. These rules were imposed on her without choice, as protection against reoccurring, deeply felt and rudely enacted injuries to her future memories yet to occur and confidences in herself to come to which she owed a measure of responsibility. No one else should compare with herself as guided mentor to her future to become a yet undetermined, fuller identity, competing against many paths of self she would choose not to become due the crude, unfair wills of others not playing well with her as a commonplace habit of shared, communal unfairness in the contests of identity.

The honest, vulnerable players become adversely affected by the rudeness of dirty gameplaying among known perpetrators rumored as bonding kindred, and everyone was a perpetrator in one style or another, leaving her little option in the end than to be more creative as necessity for precise recompenses; countering the bullying intentions of a future singularity of self being shaped by such crude motivations of style, value and the overarching lessening of a worthy, blended personality hardly felt to thrive within the embedded layers of facilitated, faded antiquity, within an excess, celestial opportunity optioned to rearward facsimile by a deadened kindness among vastly entangled, circular networks of individual survivals acting in joint coincidence of an allegedly found enlightenment.

~~

 The associating memory came back as she wandered to the captivating, privately evocative place she hadn't been back to for a long time, having determined not to be drawn back from a memorized breakage to her oftentimes relentlessly fixating query upon it, as something now a part of her beyond her willingness to choose, as group consensus focused upon her with the same gravity she found herself orbiting without recourse except to playfully spiral along with the rest, with accountable actions too deeply rooted in the historical surrender of resistance to a mocking enlightenment; but again she found herself arriving during the middle of the night ready to approach the unerodable texture of her psyche, for reality felt as the fixation of her mental practices and sensory beliefs of occurrences as the reality to appear for her benefit as much as the benefits available were shared by all others with the same fixations upon a physical world with spiritual undertones and impulsive aims.

She stood alone before her idea of the world, as she could only have said to Josh near a fire in the mountains, high from a shared joint, "imagine a world where someone stood in enlightenment before the rest as bowing witness, however that grand stance expresses itself, a few people at points in a world's long cycling inheritance find something worth calling illuminating to the rest of them during an occasional epoch of ancient time. But afterwards, the same world, trying to emulate the same illuminating enlightenments of a few from the past, finds it unattainable for the succeeding many, after long violent endeavor of wearisome historical effort, so inevitably the original enlightened ones become the excuse for a newer, mainstream perversion of it as they try to reach the unattainable. Imagine a world in which this perversion lasts centuries and millennia of toiled missteps following a few *ones* which existed solely for the moment to hold alone as a gem of time and occurrence, as a singular, abnormal discovery not meant for the many to find within group demands veiling its truth. Not meant for the future it arrives within, but precious to the moment it occurred long gone."

"What truth?"

"If, say, that imagined world lasted until this real world in time how could we know? Unless it gets illuminated again and we happen to be there in coincidence to see it," as she fell silent further staring into the shapes of the night's skylit dimness.

~~

Rey had gotten dressed with only a few infesting words aimed at her as he left as an end to a game, toppling his king piece with a forceless flick of a finger surrogated with the door closing behind him as the exit from her life for good except accidentally spurned by an uncovered future. His affections had just as quickly faded with her rudely worded countering, though he had caught her sudden and unprepared with his intolerable emotional outburst ruining her mood like a rerunning film she must watch again. In a different situation, on another night, it might have turned out differently. The abruptness of the moment had overwhelmingly afflicted her as a renewed challenge to her identity from her environment, a "here we go again" moment making her tend to analytically ramble rather than become further exposed as vulnerable through the expanding, unswerving exchanges of crudity.

Often, she had risky encounters in the city due her compelled, brave disposition to impulsively follow her intuitive tendencies, imitating her instinctive curiosity of nature as a wandering child, as if the two were the same, and she challenged herself to experience the disparity in emotive, intense contrast she could only do by involvements beyond the books she read as a teen stirring her to study the world with an ensuing loss of its seriousness as a challenge to overcome in the budding individual she attempted to foster as sighted to become with discipline.

She found the urban confidence bewildering, since it held so little substance, and such a minor connection with its origin, as if a reinvented jungle without the deft passions. A world filled with participants believing themselves overcome and lucky while without true skills or devotions beyond a usual mix of assorted, achievable victories from distant pasts as the courage of commonality to adhere to and find to surpass as the truer colors of ascendancy loudly proclaimed equally attainable without the wasted, lighted efforts of individual enlightenments in favor of a wide, manifold dimness.

"They are mostly ripe to be taken advantage, if I were inclined that way, but still ripe for advantage by many others highly inclined that way," she had scrawled somewhere and later forgotten where she had put it.

She thought that a species telling itself it was advanced in natural stature against a cosmic backdrop within an urban fitness should have greater confidence of assurance, and she had told Josh in the mountains during a fireside talk, "if we aren't advanced as a species, we should stop thinking and talking ourselves that way; if we are advanced, we should start thinking and acting as ourselves that way," under the full depth of the nightly celestial spectrum ironic in stars and the contoured shape of the galaxy they sat within near a small burning flame for warming comfort, witnessing such a feat without sensory engulfment and cerebral abandon to an abruptly collapsed, closed universe as the embodiment of entangled vertigo.

"Advanced in what way? In design of evolution, you must admit we have advanced fairly far as a species up to this point."

"Have we? As a body shape, we are hardly superior other than our ability to manipulate the physical world by the features of traits sown by evolution, as a reaping balance for a cleverly associating mind strategy.

"As far as physical and spiritual feats, which are in abundance throughout nature beyond our refuting ability to recognize as easily as we clearly see it in ourselves, we are far exceeded by the ingenuities and heights of the other animals and plants. Suppose if we were to transplant our body shape onto the many species within overlapping environmental templates of their own devise over however long a historical space, they would all fail, for anything designed by the niches available to the oceans, mountains, or trees, and the tiniest crevices found folded within reality with some form of ready sustenance and survivability have evolved to function by opportunities released through widespread, cumulative successes by other shapes.

"What would happen? They would all fail in a mad rush to find the paths back to former shapes in time, to evolve back to a former success no longer functional with human anatomy and with former niche ingenuities suddenly useless. Except the humans, newly helpless and alone without the other species now changed to defeatist shapes, trees with branches like arms, fingers and a crowning head, a cheetah inhibited by suddenly running bipetal, but so does its prey, now all and everything configured by our chosen, grand design as the fittest, telling design, until the only differentiation is size and the measuring swiftness of starvation floating the oceans and landscapes.

"You see, we are nothing except extinct without the context of nature and its diversity of niche enlightenments, we lose our sciences, our imaginations, until we try to stand upright, isolated in proven spirit and emaciated body.

"We aren't really bodily advanced as a species if we are a simple reconfiguration of traits the same as other species, using the environment as the enlargement of our traits, as the means of maneuvering the physical world, the same here and differently similar in other universal scales or everywhere else in the likely cosmos. As with our fingers," she had displayed with feigned pride at her long, thinly extending digits, "the physical world must be touched, grasped, and consumed for energies and the pleasures of new sensations, but fingers aren't everything, and everything can't have fingers," she humbled.

"I get your point. But we have fine-tuned an advancing niche," Josh countered with a seeing smile to the night at Sela's exasperation over her perspective contrary to the reality she finds surrounding her, her opinions reawakened by the mountains and the sights and sensitive moods of the mountains into a colorful frenzy of striving temper unleased by the fuel of the pit's fire and the heavy herbs they smoked.

"A species assumes its recognition of self-image as its consciousness advances for its simple niche capacity to do so, continuing the same path without much alternative or option," Sela continued.

"Can't we claim ourselves that way as justification?" Josh knew better than to try and debate Sela in the excited cerebral mood she was in but enjoyed sitting back as the welcoming victim of her charging verbiage enthralling the night and his unruffled heed of her rapidly inflecting voice.

"Sure, we can claim whatever we choose to justify ourselves, and we obviously have done that for long spans of habit, but it's not so much the imagined recognition as the demanded ownership of survival."

"Haven't we done that? It was brutal doing it, but it's done. Didn't we claim it? Don't we own and command it?"

"Command what? Ourselves?"

"Yes, and nature."

"Sure, make it the universe too," Sela laughed, "we command it all. The reason we once thought the earth was the center of the universe was because we thought we were its center, by selective capacity to do so and the silence of resistance to its idea."

Sela extracted from the relics of the world's history as emblems of record, through the ability of her obliged words over those of others gifted with silence, exactly where this essential, gaining resistance originated as an underlying, quieting force of that history, in the elixir of nature's unquenchable admiration for symmetries as a diverse compulsion of life's quest.

"We own our consciousness from the shape of our body and ensuing actions as associations, but not the ownership of an advancement so much as a kind of rebirth," she furthered.

"Rebirth, like we've done it before?"

"No, rebirth as in it's not only about us and our proper advancement as being the alleged absolute one, but about something advancing and emerging new similar to what has been countlessly done before."

"Is there another species as advanced, really?"

"I don't think that's an appropriate question to finding a manifolded perspective of reality. It's not about *another* in the competition for extinction, but the indebted relationship to all the others missing as we decide *less* to be a measured relationship proper to the force of nature contrary to ourselves. We can't truly claim ownership of a consciousness advanced in isolated recognition before the celestial ocean as if a claimed ownership for all in infinity. There is no privilege in standing alone. I don't see advancement in that perspective of a designed universe. A consciousness with such advancement is little more than the light of a mirrored reflection staring back in unused pride, even if it can describe itself wondrously and poetically as the contrary in sureness of that staring reflection's admirations.

"The thing is, if a species were conscious as we claim ourselves, but not truly advanced, as subjective as that is to find, it would be an evolutionary benefit to believe itself better suitable as a supreme skill, without the overarching influence of that disillusion occurring over millennia until an endgame never closely approached until now. The species inevitably becomes disadvantaged to cope by the success of its ranging abnormalcy," she contagiously laughed.

"People can spend their entire lives striving over a thing called love, because of a first, early, impression, or the societal urging to do it, without ever really knowing what it is except in themselves. Even if they really do have the ability to feel it, they find no outlet or true use for it except as a ready source of desperate disenchantment," she wrote the night before and kept it in her pocket until after Josh had retired to sleep, holding it between her fingers as she gingerly illuminated its tarnished transparency of bold letterings against the last glowing embers of the fire before reluctantly letting it loose to fall and submerge from reality as its burning belief transformed into an ephemeral white glow of mesmerized flames and sacrificial smoke.

~~

This was an inherited, hive-melding urbanite world where truths were non-translatable and abused as guilts and punishments of conscience against what can be lived with by coordinated effort as success of illusion, endured agedly beyond any honest resolve of integrity or anything imaginably contrary as emblem to faithfully follow except as martyring symbol of journeying exile.

She was disappointed in her lack of courage over hastily reconnecting with Neal after the prior few stoic years she had spent without looking for sexual urgency as comforting motive, recombining herself by the self-exclusion of any further idea of mutual intimacy she had long discarded as an unusable path to follow. It proved to her over agonizing years unaccompanied by her weakened confidence and the undeniable assailing of her deep-rooted solitude that she feared the risks of living alone as a weighted stone of utter oceanic despair. She feared most how she could become easily accustomed to it as a will to life, as a growing practice of future longevity, a long-held distraction and a long, self-observed life of festering inner rifts or its equivalently unresponsive sense of quieted harmony through unremitting, desolate and self-imposed separation.

There was an emotionally self-mutilating side to her identity she needed to be cautious, the sense she dared to fear of herself as a stubborn or spiteful will for self-affliction if she ever chose to despise her surrendering self or the world's strategies enough to turn away and truly ignore her own best advice as corrupted in all contexts instead. She had to retain a measure of respect for herself, to watch over and look out for herself for lack of an alternative careful observer other than the private associations captured through the moveable world as incredible, protruding and hinting prudence to reality's foreshadow sidetracking an extracted specimen from the vast world of humankind, with symbolically salted incisions becoming too disfiguring through contact with its exhibiting spectrum of whimsical meanings as influence for an unguarded, anguished mind to help forget.

The turning away would also be a turning towards a newer, unwittingly imposed, and disciplined life without alternative if she were to meet such a future version of herself face-to-face. Separation became an oasis, a protection from new memories imposed from outside, of challenged alterations to her intimate patterns of uncontested truth, and of self-doubts and festering, age-old denials as appeasing, manifolded comforts.

She had heard the silence before, listened for it as a child between the winds and rains, during moments of stillness when the universe went quiet in the darkness. As an adult, she understood better the fear of such a silence, of where it might lead and last as grateful solitude, as a temptation to give into as the intimate, overwhelming gift of surrendering her resistance.

There was no explaining it without resorting to diagnosis or self-helping kindnesses from others supplying no further elucidation and the festering of gossiping, sighted doubts, so that social life became, reciprocal to her willful efforts to pursue it, a splintering personality conflict of roving types emancipating throughout human history the full field of worldly gambit, transforming it into a world of stated, regulated experiences as the barcoded individuality of personality unrelated to an original world of daily persistence as purpose, supplanted by a new entanglement of dramatic forces bent on further sustenance skillfully preying the vulnerabilities of reality for the realms of imposing advantage and political exchange in the social forum: through private confidences of sexuality and public verbosity as the epitomes of highest, freeing value.

~~

If she had been gentler to Rey the last night together during her final year of undergraduate school, the later repeating, stolen moments fated for her memory to recount into her future, current state of unsolicited culpability at its connotations would have missed her as a torturing experience to come from its casually simple coincidence of first occurrence.

Instead, Rey might have stayed, and she

wouldn't have discontentedly gone out into the night.

The walks returning to the same haunting place over years as a revisiting recollection of evidence for new proof would have been missed too, or at the least the images would have held different intentions and directions of context.

The lingering questions and self-doubts would have been erased and excused from her psyche as "one other thing to associate outside and beyond my self-choice as the inflictions cast by other reflections of reality beyond any scope of innovative purpose given as a right of original birth to be forced to encounter as a confronting world," she got up to scrawl down on paper, trying not to forget.

With Rey gone, still in the middle of the night, unable to sleep with her roving emotions over the ending impact of her relationship with him, she took a walk. The air smelled of dirt and the ground wet from a recent showering of rain.

Living nearby, leaving her small studio apartment, she cut across the university grounds drawn to the direction of the river valley by whatever meandering path bringing her there as an inevitable endpoint, searching the atmospheric environment of her thoughts as surrogate for her attention to the moments of the real world around her as she walked as a solitary shadow in the lateness of night without cause or search for interruption, lost to the thoughts of her moods and the implication of her inner realizations after only a diploma distance away from the coastal home she had previously known as the sole aspect of reality and humanity's place within it beyond the romanticism of books, a romanticism as exclusive and painstaking to find as the gems of exceptional fictions plucked into reality from outside its nightmarish elusion in truth for the ones creating the stories, as an otherworld she knew only as the illusions of her mind's ideas in relationship with the coincidences of fates outside books and the rustic limits of localized storytelling as social instinct to follow.

In the city, while attending school, she tried to find her own story, to script her adventure and fictional reality into an experience to carry forward as a memento of a life succeeding a sought-after feat in proper sequence. She had begun to learn such fictions were hard fought as creations of a truer reality she arrived to find living as a state of utter, unquenchable redemption in its stead, "ridden with premeditated guilts usable as commodities of exchange riven from the idled ideas of the past as success," she kept for her thoughts alone.

"This new strange world has been happening here and everywhere for a long time, and unrecognizable without proper contrast of personal experience and time enough alone with it to fully appreciate," she intuited as further argument for her quiet soliloquy secreted from the world she envisioned different than the other people living there, "provisioning for everyone's thoughts its fodder accorded the varied intersecting experiences of each within the simple cohesion of divulging a continuing survival of the same as a primary, succeeding aim of perpetrators and victims."

It was the same with her the longer she lingered within its scape of erosion upon the prior landscape she knew and had grown up alongside as lush companion and cloistered measure of herself, and mentor with no other stick worth using as gauge or advice worth listening to in alternative betterment.

This concreted world was eager for her to join in too, to follow along in compassion and admitted bewilderment of a falsely elicited cosmos out of touch with humanity and her needs no longer found in the world of nature and natural things, as an enlightened everyday resurfacing like the legendary Phoenix from the pit of its ashes day after endless day with the purpose of the next perpetually in mind as wakeful guide for the future to reoccur, and forever chasing its tail as the quest of an intimate, full encirclement trapped in changeless, hypnotic enchantment.

Instead, "a world of ownership and convoluted rebirth" impressing upon Sela's thoughts the ideas of abject association she formed with unsolicited bias into an attraction for its malleable surfaces and rewarding freedoms, for she had tried drawing its contact with alluring powers and averted staring looks at its impressive, shapely reflections and its coyness of simpler fulfillment.

Distracted by her thoughts, she reached the vicinity of the river valley without much memory of how she got there, mindlessly following the routes of practiced habit like a bird at dusk homing directly to her roost for the night after a vigorous day. Sela took unattended cues from the suggestions of her environmental customs masking any loss of direction at finding herself further than she'd gone before on an unfamiliar asphalt path poking her awareness from the preceding gravel she had scuffed her footsteps atop for more than an hour among the network of city pathways traversing the older growth trees popular alongside the banks of the river.

By whatever route she had aimlessly taken to get to the asphalt path striking her alertness, upon raising her head from her gloom she saw a dim light ahead in the otherwise darkness of the path at night closely crammed between the trees on either side with low-hanging, protruding branches keeping her to the middle with care. As she moved forward, the cracked paving became dimly illuminated with short grasses rising as vaguely reflective phosphorescence.

Sela stopped upon seeing the wooden viewing platform ahead of her marking an ending for the trail. Made with a bench and with railing walls as safety against a fall to the waters below its point of view as a vantage of the valley's river.

Listening for the approval of a lingering silence as encouragement, one old, metal covered source of light appeared to her attention from an angled corner of the railing. About to step comfortably forward, Sela froze in place, quieting everything including her ability to breathe with an unusual jolt of instinctive adrenaline pulsing her thoughts as she found in her focus, having overlooked the statuesque stillness as a fixture of the setting's backdrop, she was not alone in the night.

Standing atop the platform's railing as atop the ledge of a precipice, overlooking the darkness below, with one arm holding the greyish lumber of the pole standing as the local night's only source of light, a womanly figure hovered with her back to Sela so she could only identity the uncertain figure as the silhouette shape of a woman.

At first, Sela didn't appear to be noticed, waiting in the quiet, casting shade protective between them by staying motionless, as she tried to understand the moment into a pieced together fullness of newly awakened alarm.

Impulsively, she began to step backwards,

slowly retreating towards the better darkness and a detachment from what she had nearly disturbed occurring before she got there, whatever that was. Averting her eyes downward, she was interrupted by a soft sound piercing the night's quiet like a falling star across the night's sky.

Raising her eyes, she saw the other woman looking back at her, finding the former sound of a sob in the emotional eyes turned back to question the darkness in Sela's direction, with eyes like Sela's eyes with the same staring intention looking back in reciprocal wonderment of the mere sense of disruption caused by Sela being there as a mere suspicion, though hidden from the woman's fuller senses by her stillness in the dark of a clouded, dulled space.

Sela was stuck in time, frozen by the moment and its raging implications of choice. Looking back, the other woman was motionless, frozen spellbound along with Sela in her withdrawing stoppage of the localized moment to protect her emotional moment eagerly ready to bolt from reality rather than face it anew in the delicate shape it had formed for her private, lost viewing.

Without knowing whether the other woman truly saw her, Sela watched the woman's searching eyes only briefly finding hers, by accident, until she scanned her vicinity for long moments from her lit stance into the masked night as a simple check over her shoulder for a confirmation of aloneness.

Finally, the woman broke her stone-stillness and turned away from Sela to reface her former fate whatever it was yet undetermined; even undeterred if Sela were to succeed a quiet withdrawal into the obscurity of her denial of a journeyed destiny with a stranger.

Sela didn't need the assurance of knowing the other woman's purpose, as if not of her right to pry into another's voided spiritual journey beyond the physical specimen she saw as a stranger on a ledge having reached an end to a path with standing approval to a vantage beyond the threshold of her next step to hold her aloft.

The woman might have reached a point of utter challenge within herself because of her life and the world she inhabited, as a need to find out about herself, which Sela had no certitude to interrupt. She believed in the need and right to find abstract challenge in the world, to press the boundaries of reality, to dispel the illusions of alleged manifestations, to see for once a compelled, essential hint, an unheard utterance in reply to the forced excavation of a single soul among countless in the wide infinite outside the one.

To silently back away, she respected the other woman's solitary fate to bravely journey her choice to where it had led her before Sela's accidental pause.

Later, she couldn't tell of it or seek explanation, even though such events shape the fabrics of an overlooking reality in measured salience of experiences. There was no one besides herself as need for explanation of her transitional quest for true belief, as the stranger, within the throes of her intimate ritual, as an acceptance of challenge, with their two souls drawn precisely together through personal rapture, within a singular moment, by whatever their prior stories, and found together as an innocently shared challenge riven and energized by a joint, tugging vigor much like the strings of puppets.

Sela was bound to a fate with another woman by the mere coincidence arising from her earlier, nasty mood with Rey, and thereby doomed to the luck of everlasting mortification through her unfinished memory of a new stranger as an unforgiving, final reward.

~~

Sela stopped and stood loitering near the original branching path leading into the trees to the wooden platform, the same as the first time she walked by chance as an aimless wanderer down its shadowed route. She couldn't walk away, so veering off the path she took a quiet seat out of sight on a nearby hillside with proper view of the only exit inside the city she discovered in the night relevant to her unfortunate luck by having not remained absent as experience in her short-term memories. Instead, by continuing the straight path as an original, absentminded choice and an alternate reality, it would have inevitably led her back to her small apartment in the middle of the night, her walk having gone on long enough, and her tired mood shifted ready to enter bed for the night without rudely inserted complications to her previously private, ongoing disinterest.

Though hard to tell in the desperate attachment of first enacting awareness relating two strangers where a relationship only subliminally existed beforehand through a shared environmental milieu of sympathetic contact, the woman had looked Sela's age and a student like herself. It seemed more impossible to go back than to await the predicted abandonment of a determination, if the determination were a reality of the missed moment left to Sela's memory to reap from a naturally sown disassociation grown through her illegibility to her environment's messages torturously lost in translation during the moment, while reclaimed later in hindsight as "improper inaction," and the sense of opinion from others becoming in time carelessly concerning to her.

After a stretch of time had passed without change, Sela reasoned with bodily discomfort it was time she got up and walk away from a stressing commitment upon her mood without liability for it. Her so-thought *improper inaction* was lingering for an outcome like an intruder, a voyeur, or a criminal as nonaligned as the night itself, as a mere phantom creeping alongside the restless and sleeping plethora of people honorably enjoying more urban tenure as fitting kin to the strange woman than Sela sitting alone in the mere shadows of night hiding from the world except herself any admittance of belonging to it.

Resolved to go, she did finally get up from the ground to brush off her backside and quietly swipe her hands before she moved down the slope from her embarrassing concealment, reentered the network of pathways exactly where she had first diverted from it, and began her return home as if none of it had occurred while walking upright with the confidence of full deletion from her memories by the time she got there.

Slowly reaching the first turn of the finely graveled path leading further to the impending blockage of her sight of the dead-end path's sole exit she had kept closely within her furtive attention by incessantly looking back for a hopeful disclosure through the reemergence of the strange woman before it's too late, until Sela hesitated and finally stopped in defeat before she dared to lose sight of an inactive exiting pathway for the briefest admittance of uncertainty from which there could be no turning back once she further continued.

On the path in front of her, a single dried red leaf "twirls the breeze" into achievement of self-expression through a fleetingly simple, communicative means opportunely tied to the passing presence of Sela as symbolic gift to her moment.

She couldn't go on and not know. "I can't do that to myself as a future to readmit again and again without answer or hope of it!"

She knew *stranger* meant never seeing the other woman again.

She fully realized the implications, even in her sullied mood, of a walk into the future and away from knowing the closest truth she could muster of the outcome of an encounter with a stranger she had no real obligation to carry further as a burden upon the distending veins of her thoughts.

She lingered for a while longer, staying to the shadows of the crusted old trees with tones of differing darkness cast from spattered city lights dimly hovering in the distance and occasioned sporadically among the network of city pathways.

"I have to go back down the path again," as Sela bravely reemerged onto the gravel path from under the tree, returning in the direction of the original branching destiny causing her to miss through delay any further hope of undisturbed sleep for the night, to venture that dark asphalt path one more time to its endpoint, to check on the status of an unknown woman perhaps in a state of self-peril or maybe just out for the fun of sobbing her sorrows at the valley's edge as an imaginative, riskily exchanging void masked as the illusion of wonder better left uninterrupted by Sela and her private involvement with it as an event where conceivably she did not belong to begin with, or as a proud returning point in time questioning her careful heroics with scorn or mockery as a customary response to her cautious approach to heroism.

She approached the path to the dead-end platform again as the completion of her determined goal of the moment to reenter the splitting pathway with self-urgency, assuming it as trial for the split in her mindful resilience for the night, as the shifting challenge to her identity and resolve as Sela under examination through contorted fate. She began her trek back with a strength of will she was usually reserved as a habit in expressing, preferably keeping her strengths to herself and out of sight.

She deserved what another look might tell her as more and reveal as solution to the incomplete image previously missed in the confusion of the moment, with a new detail making better sense of it.

Either way, "enough is enough, I need completion of this!"

Now, it was for Sela's peace of mind to overcome and get past the night's disconnection roused through another's struggle with an undefined personal torment, much like a sickness in its effects like a virus slowly grabbing control of the body until overwhelmed and contagious, as Sela was trying to avoid catching in getting too close.

Already, she had given too much to a stranger as fair social exchange, so "this is for me," she contended.

"Or to take the chance to recognize a despair in another!" She suspected to have to carry that as a bind from her past to haul forward as a load of burden from an inconsiderate other person while she simply lost her way in the darkness, as accident the same as countless others have by intimately slogging the world while bereaved of its finer meanings.

There was also the real possible necessity of verbal challenge or a physical confrontation beyond her usual preference for a nonconfrontational skillset in her dealings with the world unless proper last resort in defense of an abuse against herself.

"You don't know anything yet," she encouraged herself, knowing there would likely be a simple answering outcome to satisfy her, like the potential risk of a life might be equated to the random flipping of a coin as a shameful thought to admit where only hours earlier she had no admittance of anything associated to be shocking in her thoughts beyond a usual denseness of distractions and her breakage with Rey appearing as a nonevent to her thoughts with her current predicament regretfully ongoing.

Retreating further back in the sequence of events, the same could be said for Rey's outburst of affection leading to her walking a sleepless night as substitute to an alternate future, now lost as its parallel, in which she might have continued into easy slumber if not abruptly led astray by the unsolicited, unconsented actions of others imposed upon herself "inescapably once again."

People assumed protections from readily provisioned sources, whether intimacies of family, neighborhood, city, statuses such as vehicle and gems of unearthed vision, unearned and thereby unowned tattoos, religions and traditions, customs and superstitions, giving the instinctive fear of grouped, dynamically instilled wards, all meant in one form and measure or another to protect through implied intimidations and requested violence as practiced answer, inclusive of rendering self-inflictions and improper readings of convoluted meanings.

She and the stranger shared a belief, extracted through a briefness of insignificant moments together, lived it as experience and chose the freed outcomes open for each to respectfully expound further at whatever cost as a conjoined destiny of two women drawn as strangers to a point to act out a drama within a singular roving instant of reality as stage for a related experience of the cosmos to later disentangle into a composed morality the same as endlessly reoccurred throughout a history.

The conflict of another's suffering contested to her own as relevance.

"This is where I have a problem," with the discontent of another rudely left for Sela to try to pry an unanswerable solution, with the potential of a future lessened by riddled abandon of the insoluble never reclaimed through the utter hopelessness of a lost chance as a desperate sympathy to embrace from the next day forward as an uncalled-for aspect of her freshly cut identity as sensitive and woundable.

As she approached closer to the branch in the pathway leading back to her former, unfinished fate, she was trying to fulfill the urge to reclaim a lost chance not originally belonging to her.

"I have to go back and live it either way," with fresh determination to take the path back to the platform to eavesdrop on a total stranger in the middle of night to "make sure she is right within a proper spectrum of mind."

Individuals should arise within this atmosphere of fearful guardedness as unprotected, undefended, and vulnerable in impending isolation against the world's heavier enactions.

"Here is the reason I wander sleepless at night, the thing I try to avoid," without victimizing herself in the process as she was not in the need to do as increased disorder upon her self-awareness. "Now I have to go and confront it, forced to make a scene if necessary, twice in one night."

Over the last few years, she had gradually relinquished this place as a growing practice until there was nothing left except to leave it behind once school was finished, to pack it away in an attic chest as old souvenirs for her suspected future to find again if she wanted as something new to reclaim.

The entangled state of connected reality between humanity and its environments should have orchestrated countless such dramas throughout history going back through millennia as the first urges of a malleable reality took shape in an advancing, aware species designed by nature to endure all except its multiplicity in common, hidden as shadows in the plain light of a private, esoteric reality and the eventual fade of memory into dust not to reemerge.

Why was Sela so culpable? Simply because she shared a minimal light in the middle of the night with another woman's desperation brought on over years, with Sela only making her appearance in the woman's story at the very end, taking on the role of a hidden, mysterious stranger or even nothing more than a hint of a presence like an unseen, caressing apparition.

In that case, she was equally to blame for all the others "for the mere reason of a source of shared light!"

Instead, she preferred seeing this world of reinvented reality and premeditated answer of choice as concrete, and merely ephemeral in its secret, unseen indiscretions.

With the audible scuff of a sliding footstep on gravel, the other woman abruptly appeared before a spooked Sela just as she approached and was about to veer into the darkness to find her, closely occurring so she had to sidestep to avoid the woman as she speedily bypassed.

Sela took a simple glance at the other woman enough to see her distraught state, her solitude, and her confidence at exiting the dead-end pathway leading to the wooden platform with a vertigo vantage of the falling river valley when standing atop the flat top of the platform's rail, with the pole of a light for support against the otherwise emptiness of existence in its pure, isolated despair.

For a split moment, as the other woman

first came before Sela out of the drearier darkness within the dimly light they closely shared for a prolonged instant, the woman hesitated while looking up to see Sela strangely there, as if stopped not by surprise but by the question of an embarrassing recognition as she appeared to briefly deliberate whether to act, according to decorum of telling appreciation, on that sight as an obligation Sela also didn't share as custom. Instead, seeing the moment better, she turned away to hide the encounter as forgotten from the ripe light of reality as a new light of another day approached to conceal in glowing bustle a lush and restless primal jungle readily apt for the ancient task of advancing a coinciding persistence of knotting, constricting entanglements.

Only a few minutes later, alone on the path in the late hours of night, Sela halted her steps with a first deeply recurring breath of cool, uninterrupted air filling her lungs once more, reenergizing her as she repeatedly blinked her eyes to her vision blurred in watery restraint, leaving her for long moments motionless until the threshold had broken and she had deftly smeared the wetness of each cheek, releasing her to look around, regain herself and continue home.

Later, Sela had to reconsider with a tinge of unfinished wonder, "did she sense I was there before in the dark, unmoving, as a further presence touched through the communicative information of the environment available even then with the last fraying strings of hope holding you above the depriving void of last choice?"

Sela said goodbye to any further elucidation by leaving the city after her graduation a few months later with the expectation of not returning, at least not for a long time or for extended periods of time, only to find herself a few months afterwards back to the city as her urban refuge from the unexpected consequence of collapsing fates during the upcoming summer months back home again.

In the city, there was the shared, coincidental illusion of not being alone, making it feel safe and encouraging to her species.

CHAPTER 4: ANTIQUATED BEACH

The distinct, hollow grinding of rocks beneath her footsteps textured into a reacquainted memory of a solitary child accustomed to the soft, moveable uttering as daily, overlooked occurrences of guttural vocals and as throwable, smoothly aiming projectiles with ample temporal opportunity to use for playthings for her rising imaginations instilled by the trees, the reoccurring waters, the birds and other local voyeurs attentive of a fledgling girl having become the flawed woman stepping again atop the colored dreams of her youth.

Walking out from the thick trees either side of the slender path she excitedly followed more from old practice of recurring memory than visual cue, the tall grasses and reeds tenderly caressing her bared arms, legs, and sliding through her fingers as she grasped at gritty, bending strands, she saw again for the first instance, along with Josh behind her as a first sight, with the approaching salted scent rousing a sensual curiosity to contracted anticipation, the abruptly opening expanse of beach, ocean and forest merging in solitary, uncontested symmetry, complete with the squawking spray of gulls lifting from the shore's edge mirroring the local forest birds which had been actively signaling around her homecoming, and an unprotecting, cooler wind persuasively gliding over her sensitive skin.

Josh followed in her steps until they sauntered onto the rocks of the antiquated beach unfettered through relative isolation, much as anything natural remaining in the world as a concept of modern reality had become strangely antique to Sela's first impression of it freshly unlike any earlier sense rising from her experience of it in the past.

She visualized the beach as a disappearing, fading vision of a past, the dream of a former life thoughtful and long dead.

Sela realized she was emotional not solely for the homecoming and her rekindled senses of a familiar atmosphere owned of a different aura of quiet from what she'd become accustomed living in the city, but also for its impending loss through her personal defeat and that of steadfast others not unlike herself in sensitivity to it as a choiceless, choking thing to turn away from as a personal context of obligation.

He had travelled with her the two-day trip to the coast, intending to help make ready the house she'd been away from for years and deprived for too long of intimate habitation. After the out-ing to the mountains, Sela decided she couldn't make valid choices anymore from the urban visage standpoint she had been living too long. She had gotten the experiences she needed when she first made the choice seven years earlier to go there. She needed to return to the only home she knew, itself with its associated, slanted memories. She was confident in her return, detached by the anguish of lost involvements, discordances of the past, and the distances of time contrary to a closing future.

For Josh, the winding drive supplied depth to Sela's identity as a context he hadn't found before, pried to learn as details or much imagined from the telling of her fixed, withheld memories she'd kept silent about over the few years he'd known her, obviously explaining ahead of time as a method of preparing him for what lied ahead in her predicted exposition of herself before him through inevitably seeing the museum of her childhood. She had never requested any fair explanation in return from him, but the drive to her coastal home fated the involvement of his senses in her past life and a naturally curious imagination for things already done.

During the trip, she explained about herself through long-held recollections not previously spoken to anyone else and impulsively recalled aloud, for she wanted to justify and give background to what he would find out about her through his senses and private insights once they arrived, forcing her to reveal as they approached closer a self-interest not usually freely offered. She was more active than usual with her willingness and enthusiasm for starting the conversation with unusual focus upon herself and her memories of the place they were headed.

"They were private people, preferring to avoid the world after having lived in it for so long, after tiring of its blatancy and empty redundancy as I understand better now having lived it myself," she said without consideration of offence to Josh, herself and everyone they might know for living the same, for he enjoyed Sela as always for her usual careless outbursts of truth, accepting his hapless involvement in the make-up of the world as something he recognized for what it really was alongside her in opinion, and as something he couldn't much change as a self-sacrifice to retaining or refreshing its fading achievement.

She continued, "they had already retired from that life before they came to where we are going. Already in their fifties by then, they had found a sterile, plump success. Sometimes, I think I was a future access to the world for them, to not fully lose themselves to the world they left behind as no longer a fitful one. As I grew, I'd be compelled to venture out, or them with me, bringing back to them a contact and connection not otherwise desired to further pursue. I was a sanctuary from the desperations of a predicted loneliness together.

"And they couldn't resist me, once they decided to find me, just for the impulsive desire for a focus of affection and renewing companionship. I became a source of inspired passions as a child can be. I can understand their fateless choice now for an alternative they made then, with the fuller appreciation of fathoming what they looked for in coming here for an escaped life."

"Fateless?"

"Sorry, again, my perspective in hindsight. It's better to say, I can see the world they must have seen then, and I can understand the lack of alternatives they had for themselves in such a state of a world they lived with over years before truly rationalizing it more appropriately as an influence upon life to best retreat and overcome. But how? At times, I've come to ask the same question, and ponder the alternatives as unanswered riddles in the eternal quest for a meaning of substance more than a mere intangible faith or unfaith as believable contact of a living existence by its curious, temporal inhabitants," when Sela gave to a brief silence, realizing she'd been talking on as if to herself.

She was living a similar retreat now as they did then, and she overheard it sounded in her words to Josh, so she turned to him and smiled to dismiss herself as ordinary.

Josh had a strange questioning look when

she eyed him with her smiling defense, before he queried, "temporal?"

"Yes," she further explained, "as each person is limited by the perceptive scale and knowledge of the shortened time-period they happen to chance live in, very unfortunate and torturously to some sensitive enough to it as a difference unlike to others, and each time the relative same," and she blurted a laugh at the eternal conundrum repeating itself in renewed shapes and impulses of a long traversed history getting her into a position to emerge as Sela into this world as a state of reality to reside and a spontaneous choice already predetermined an endlessness ago.

Sela and everyone else were only found through the situation of "our individual descriptions of it as a life of active or inactive choices entangled within the world of premediated choices dangerously established as a differing context of experience."

Mostly, Josh preferred quietly listening to Sela's opined associations of the world without debating her so much as careful prodding to insight her bigger picture.

"The spring after my first year was when I inherited the place," she offered.

"You mentioned before, they both passed the same spring, that must have been a challenging time for you," Josh euphemistically sympathized with her, as different as it was to attract and reveal a sympathy to Sela on a personal, verbal parallel due her plain disenchantment with such normalized sympathies. When the opportunity arose, he tried with her as best he could, and listened first as preference, though it often seemed she didn't really expect it as a custom for herself and managed to continue without true offense for its absence. It didn't appear odd to her.

"Yeah, really either way they would have gone closely together, after one died the other was bound to die soon after if not killed in unison the first time by some accident. You'll see when you get there and imagine living it a bit as an everyday willpower of endurance in isolation, but it's a hard place to leave to go back to the new world once you've lived it awhile, and even harder to stay alone with its full display of memories gawking back at your solitude like a lingering sympathy to the daily practice of your defeat as a toiling, absurd and lasting spirit.

"Henry couldn't see me ever returning for permanent, except for visits to this remoteness we're heading to as a setting to call home as one way of describing it, but otherwise with just the place as companion left to endure alone, it was too sad a state to have to admit to live. There was no future left, years bequeathed ahead in expectation had abruptly been erased for him in an instant with the swift stroke of a command, beckoned by the world to witheringly stare at and to have it stare back at his humiliation in trying contrast before its command upon him, and the growing conflict of a tested spirit for the amusing benefit of the cosmos. Henry had too much pride for that, so good for him, I guess."

Sela encouraged the belief of a better death being correctly fitting for Henry as seemingly cold but also with a deeper, bitter empathy Josh heard behind her insinuating words and distant stares as she described the world around her with the descriptions as she withstood it to be. When he managed, he saw the truth in her direct eyes if not her words and illegible looks *beneath* normalized reactions as he'd learned to expect of people and only discovered of himself through knowing her.

Josh's natural habit of mind persuaded his thoughts to quietly beg the question to ask aloud, "didn't you love him?"

Henry was an adopting father whose passing she eased into the conversation with the plain cheering comment "good for him," which to anyone not knowing Sela better would be construed through hearing it to be as an obvious flaw in her character. For Josh any association of such conducts of reacting within the bounds of normalcy were dismissed as inapplicable in relationship to his friend, and she was not to be too harshly judged for nonexistent emotional reactions rather than ones textured differently, even beyond his perceptive ability to properly sight with confidence.

It was strangely inspiring how she talked of the world as if motivated in her beliefs of it through a habit Josh admittedly never truly felt himself, at least not in the same steadfast way when she wasn't around.

"You think the cosmos ordains such things so fatefully?"

"What else would?"

For a while they continued in silence before she uncharacteristically broke it again while Josh listened, occasionally gazing sideways to her as mute sign of attention, not that she noticed his looks as she pried further into herself.

"Not me, and not the Henry I knew before, but the one he saw ahead of him perhaps if he longer, further lingered among the familiar world he didn't want to learn to regret or further fathom as a solitude. It's only the rare individual to withstand the tortures of solitude for any true measure of uncertain time. It was brave of him to embrace his death and permit it to overwhelm him as a better alternative, a solution he owned without surrendering."

After a silence, Josh interrupted with his unchecked query, "so it would have been surrendering for him, you think, to live on?" Josh suddenly felt he was fortuned to hear from a heartfelt Sela a previously unheard, personal eulogy for the man Henry she had known as a father and kept silent about until then, while reciprocally she externally appeared indifferent to it as a transpiration and the confusion of simple misconstructions of unheeded expectation on his part as expecting listener.

"I think so, he could only have become less than the individual he was before, never better again in his eyes. I don't think most have the constitution and will for long suffering in the company of solitude, it simply breaks them down into a caricature of a former self rather than in the end a self-affirmation with enlightened perspective. Only in the rare, the very few people, genetically prone, does it become a practice intended at making an individual become stronger, allowing them to overcome into newer realms of experience the vast multitude can only contend through small, paced dosages of chance at self-denials, angers and pent resentments at the abusive uncertainty of it all as a final achieving endgame to claim."

~~

"I used to wander through these woods and walk this length of beach as a kid. There was nothing else as things to do much of the time, and such a thing to do was fittingly gifted as a child's ambition to explore can be," shortly waving her arm in a gesture encompassing the entirety of the forest stretching far and high inland. "This stretch and vicinity of it near the beach was my playground, the branches of trees the metal bars, and this rocky beach was my sandbox."

"It's an impressive location, beautifully secluded." It was Josh's first walk on the pebbled, stony beach. They had walked for longer than an hour before reaching an impassable jutting cliff at high tide merged with the frothy, breaking waves.

"During low tide, you can access a beach farther on, the other side, by walking under the cliff faces. Otherwise, we'd have to go over, through the forest and a lot of rough climbing," as she explained the vicinity to him like how she might explain her dream awakening her during the night, allowing the images to flow, echo and bounce the symbolic realm of wakeful reality for truer meaning associated specific to her.

"The beach is neatly cut off at high tide," Josh alleged, stopping to scan the length back from where they had walked since they turned at its vocal tidal endpoint of thrashing water on rock and begun returning the walk back to the secluded home.

"Getting here by beach, yes, but you'd have to be properly motivated, for it's a long walk, but there are other, shorter ways."

"Does anyone ever come here?"

She hesitated before answering, "no," keeping the untruth composed quietly within where it belonged to stay, "the remoteness keeps it mostly silent of other people or the direct influence of the world," her wavering voice concealed by the ocean winds racing to give chorus to the trees, she gingerly looked to him with an imitating smile she quietly, privately abhorred before releasing it, turning away to stare at the ocean between the strands of her gusting hair. "Sometimes, you see boats go by."

"And animals?" Josh turned to scan the length of forest rising from the beach's edge into a thickness of old grown evergreens made to slant at an angle from the perpetual chiseling force of wind and rain.

"Well, there are those, not just the gulls. The forest has its own fill of bodies and mix of identities same as everywhere else does, jungle, forest or city," not wanting to expound those incredulous stories truly intimate to herself as an intensifying philosophy of her own mystical relationship to contend as validity's temptation in the proving game of reality.

"It's amazing all this stretch of beach was just for you and your family."

"Adopted family."

Then, "family," softer with her new correction, "mostly for me to play with as a backdrop, they were older and didn't come down here as often, except for walks together with me at times, one or the other or both, and to see the sunrises when motivated to look for inspiring encouragement. You must come down and see a few early sunlit rises before you head back."

"All the smooth stones deposited here," he interjected, "it's really an incredible spot, a long, curling cove. They picked this spot for the house since the beach ends here, I guess, sheltered away."

"As a girl, I used to wonder where all the rocks came from. I imagined them placed here one at a time, once a day with the tide, for an eternity before I arrived, just for me to find when I did, with each one carefully placed according to an unseen, random formula. They were an artful work in progress over eons by the hand of persistent tides as a forceful, ancient geoglyph gifted to the sky by the waters, an ever-changing, never-finished toil of a truly precious, explicit work of the finest, purest art. I got to be a detail in the design when I lay prone or sat on the rocks for extended periods, blending with the picture, sitting or standing within it, which I often did, staring back at the sky to see it looking back and smiling through the clouds or some other symptom of imagination."

As they were heading back following the beach to the path leading to the house, she led him on a deviated route until she stopped at a nearby intended spot, "I fell from up there, and landed here, in the rocks," she pointed at a spot in front of them indistinguishable from any other spot on the beach.

"You fell from up there?" He peered upward from the base of the exposed, layered, naturally grounded wall marking the edge of the beach farthest from the ocean and the end of the rocks.

He recalled shortly before when they departed looking down from the grassy edge above him then, a few steps off the overgrown path they had tracked getting there from the house, with a shudder of vertigo as he had leaned forward to gauge the depth below before Sela gently pulled him back by the hand to follow her, thereby breaking the spell of his curiosity, telling him, "there's another safer path we could have taken, but I thought you'd like the view."

It was the first instance they walked to the beach after arriving, "this way is winding and it's grown narrow in my absence," she explained as he became growingly awestruck by the scented panorama of the approaching beachscape.

"And snatched from the air by the palm of the rocks there," she carefully pointed just in front of where they stood, at the same smooth, colored stones littering the inner beach. "I guess the rocks saved me, or at least stopped my acceleration, as another way of looking at it."

"That's incredible," with full astonishment as he looked once again incredulously upward at the height to the ledge and downward to the rocky floor near his feet.

"Good thing the rocks are smooth. I wasn't incredibly old. Only about here I guess," indicating with her outward stretched hand, leaning sideways slightly, to the height of her knee, "softer at that age, I guess."

For long moments they stood in silence. There were no proper words to the revealing moment happening between them. Sela had no memory of the event, having been told vocally at a much later age, while he was hearing it the first instance, leaving him with no further answers than her to the racing questions inspiring his amazement at her incredulous story of a collapsing, traumatic reality nonchalantly exposed as a past occurrence of her hushed inner world.

She stood, surprised at herself for having told the story, for she hadn't intended on telling anyone, giving away her relaxed trust in Josh in the moment, resisting her impulses to give too easily to others as genuine rule for herself due to an unruled reciprocation and lack of fair exchange ordinary as a coarse charisma of the world in wild, ample distribution of contorted freedoms of distrust.

"Were you injured? I mean, obviously nothing visibly," he offered her for lack of a desired reply at the implied gossiping suggestions of her anecdote fueling his thoughts with forced constraint.

After a pause, "surprisingly, no. Not that I remember any of it, only whatever I was told later. It's incredible really, all that height and not a broken bone. I learned of it by accident just like how I think I've surprised you with it. I don't know too many more details. I expect the quiet was to conceal some form of guilty belief of fault, or perhaps to not have to admit mine for recklessly falling."

She didn't mention the detail she chose to omit, "the fall was a symptom, not the cause of a later effect, but the effect itself. The cause was in me before the fall," though she silently accepted it as an accidental incident due her inexperience with the world no different than any other child under two years of age.

"They must have lived with a measure of blame for it," she imagined aloud as a manifold memory signifying her detachment to it during her upbringing as an implanted retention causally related to her solely through the telling experiences of others as a brave willingness to tell. She assumed the quiet anguish of the guilt in another over an action for which she was likely the one of sole culpability for her curiosity, "as much as the infant of the time could be made responsible for her active misdeed, leaving truly no fault to affix other than an accident prone reality in which we all live in through coincidence with those pitfalls," before she added aloud for Josh, "in the end, it was no more than an event with mixed emotions, none mine. No one else knows except you now, and I will not likely really need to share it again," she confessed, "just the once," before she turned to lead him back to the path to the house, leaving any shame for herself or anyone else behind with the rocky spot she never should have pointed out: with the blame in her unchecked excitement.

"Thank you, Sela, for the confidence you show in sharing that with me," he encouraged her with an arm across her shoulder.

"Maybe I shouldn't have told you. It's sounds more serious telling you aloud than it really was, since I have no memory of it, so no harm done. It was worse for them, living with the knowledge of it afterwards. I didn't appreciate it much before, a bit selfishly as I think of it now. I think I told you because it was really their experience, not mine, as a way of describing them to you."

Sela felt the sharp pangs of regret for her self-abusive honesty in relating stories from her memories, with her way of simply describing the eventful pasts which came to mind to tell as they appeared before her, from the fact of her senses bombarded by her return to her home, its familiarity and private reappearances coupled with the idea of her own undisciplined lack of control in telling it aloud to another person when she knew it could have been kept silent forever as a vow without the need to vocalize her intimate details; while trying to mute a heightening passion inadvertently focused upon herself.

It was hard to avoid with Josh, but she hadn't intended on revealing much of herself to another person, to show her childhood self like this on exhibition through the escaped local details stirring her symbiotic memories and released to someone else and the air whispering it to the trees and the birds to rumor upon, to stir the same forgotten remembrance of localized pains, like a naked exposition of entrails or a portrait for art she was nude modelling before a stranger's eyes, for she felt a bit towards him as a stranger with her being the one exposed in plain view through an exchange of charity without expected recompense.

"We have so many ceremonies decorating ourselves for our feats, awards and glories of physical achievements and newer world records, and it all pales when compared to the simple feats experienced as a participating witness to this beach and all that occurs here of which I observed but a fair smidgen. And this is one spot, one location, manifolded globally as an exhibition of unawareness to be feasted upon if chosen to prefer the minimalized, spotlighted feats of one, such as the brave Olympian heroes," she smilingly explained with a laugh together at the end. "We contain but a hint of the spectacle of physical awarenesses capable as skills, far exceeded by nature in its feats of maneuverable dexterities and reachable strengths, unless collectively ignored as the rambling, soulless and *terrorizing* monopoly of nature properly boycotted from competition," emphasizing the absurdity of her words through the deriding inflection offered as loudness above the thrusting winds.

He was only staying for less than two weeks before she would remain on her own for the summer or however long she stayed as a future decision not yet made; and it was Josh having earned her confidence to further describe herself, at least during these moments while he was with her at her house and within its borders; she was without anything else serious enough to distract her during his stay with her as a sympathy she might *look* to want to beg by her self-centered utterances, and without the invading reward in turn of his memories surrounded by the source of his private visions of childhood exhibited for her in plain sight to dissect.

The sighted space of beach and ocean, and

sky and forest were enclosed upon her private individuality, and haunting in its prior absentia of urbanized styling long before Josh knew her as he came to freshly see, in better context and fuller texture, the deeper aspect of her previously opined, overlooked personality.

In everything, she had no choice except to dwell on the future according to her past relationships with its looming, alerting conveyances, seeking the mentorship of her memories. In this way, by better predicting her future outcomes, she better understood her placement within the past with higher confidence walking the present in dragging watchfulness and abundant caution.

"By the time I knew her, she had new beliefs, they both did, or they wouldn't have gone so remotely to here as a place they hadn't known to live before. They knew me longer than I knew them. I had a shorter interval near the end, after all those suckling years of youth. But it was more the idea of feeling at first, and later as I was older and knew them better, it fostered into a way of life for them, hidden away in their belief."

"What did they believe?"

"I don't know, maybe just in me, maybe I'll find it myself someday and figure it out to see then. I must believe isolation teaches something hard to describe without the steady enthusiasm of its memorized experience in the aches of your body and mind. You must be prepared for it, and they were determined in their contention to face it. To do it, they needed me, so they found me, the best available contender, and brought me along for the journey."

~~

Near the house, there was seldom any wind, the air calm as she remembered it from living there as a child. Sometimes, it would gustily blow through the long-swaying, upper leafy branches billowing while she watched calmly from the ground with stilled air closely surrounding her under warming light.

She was fearless before nature in all her coupling experiences with it as a flowing aspect of reality. Even when pressed with an overwhelming sense for the lighted presence of danger, she would transform to acute stillness like the air around the house as a viewable reflecting presence with the pious mimicry of a trusted, spirited confidant recklessly listening in closely coinciding belief.

She needed to find constant distraction from herself, even a simple interference such as seeing, like habitual trances or a spinning top held in timeless balance for the lengths she sustained it, though she never could for long enough the same as everyone, to attend to her focus while avoiding the compulsive obsessiveness luring her towards old habits by seeking new ones to entertain her rousing emotional states. The avoidance of mindful distractions broke the enchantment of her torrential thoughts like a sun beaming through a crack in the clouds only momentarily before lost to the shade again with its closing blink.

She was intending to remove herself from the vicinity and influence of others, the plan willfully thought out as dreaded fantasy to endure for a future. Naturally, she doubted the choice to extendedly stay in the house as a surfacing aspect of her growing idea of fear, an idea unlearned previously from her youthful time with nature animated around her beach world as a confident playmate. Instead, it came to her later, suddenly without the attached comforted livability of easy acceptance as it comes at once to unsuspecting others into an approved, cathartic style of life at an early age.

Instead, Sela meant to learn it better, intending to overcome the thoughts controlling her called "fear" as she learned the truer meaning of it, lingering as a trailing path in her memories from its entrance in her past with her first initiations with people and relentlessly infiltrating her thoughts with closer frequencies the more experience she amassed into her predicted future state reflecting back in the closing embrace of the house and its adjacent ocean world with its influence of caressing mystery as solace.

By then, she knew she was barely influenced by *fear* as an emotional condition similar or to the extent of the rest of her species by the opinion of her experiences, perhaps from not having felt it as a developing child to know, or else through a genetic anomaly as can be common among a few within any diversity of expression such as "a broadly distending species reaching into every niche of nature to impure by its steady hand," having misplaced the note it was written on.

Sela knew the fear had already found its way to her isolated beach like how it reached its human tentacles everywhere else as the finality of a contest beyond her natural wonder for it, without the prior foresight to know it as a dying approach as it impedingly slouched forward towards a coaxing, beckoning future.

Even after a few days, she could sense her emotions again simply from inhaling the scented winds and the whispers of relinquished memories, seeing the daily subtle changes of the clandestinely embedded setting she had omitted from her life for years as a repressed memory she didn't want to contest. She had begun to reclaim possession of its attuned and tangled belief, seeing the world again through her younger, childish eyes.

Through the recurring acuities of her freed, reborn senses and cautiously youthful spirit in Josh's company while initially rejoined with the extremer thresholds through her reborn sensitivities gained from the wind's coolness on the beach that time of year, giving her a cultivated sense of pride or a *high* beyond the joints they occasionally smoked.

She had begun to sensually uncover in waiting her emotions unwearyingly there in the trees and stones, the air and the waters, the flora and animals wildly spiraling its coiling determination to which she affixed as a claimed relationship with an emotively complicit nature by having lived together before in agreement and rearing, much like family must feel to those with large enough jungles of familial experiences to suffice as surrogate for a crucial devotion to inspire an emotively similar *"high of reunion,"* as Sela unkindly whispered when alone while dismissed as "the incertitude of choice to predict your own impending betterment or fated doom."

The caressing experiences of being back in the house, walking the beach and breathing the salted air, the same as in the mountains or any natural settings not yet fully siphoned of spirit, or alone with the singularity of reality in momentary isolation, she found the constant devotion of a renewed, mentored confidence proudly welcoming her back and setting eyes on her again while radiating a curious wonderment at her having left.

~~

She wanted to confess into a cohesive story her irrevocable memories of the beach from the last time she was living in the house, also the first and only time she tried spending the full summer in her home alone, as an intimate anecdote worth boldly retelling. She came close with Josh a few times during vulnerable moments, and she was glad later to have checked her trust before going too far with her loose words, even to the point of his voluntary inclusion as an unwitting accomplice. It would have been careless to include him and destructive to her reason for being back at the coastal house, or one of the reasons for her coming back as an obstacle to overcome for her significance to continue in self-worth, to achieve her worth-saving confidence through sating her doubts as a finality to reach and a relinquishing finished conclusion by whatever detrimental endgame result must be faced.

She felt shamefully predisposed of a fruitless need for sympathy with Josh as a remarkably trustworthy person beyond the unusual pale of people. Especially, she existed without having to further elaborate herself with him as a grateful preference to her differing nature in the exploit of emotions as reviving sustenance or kinship. Sela maintained an implied impunity by not being endlessly drawn to spotlighted questions satisfying another's exposure to hidden curiosities latently waiting to be unearthed from her familial environment as disobedience to another light of a different place as one more accustomed and gleaning brighter.

Josh respected her secrecy and didn't pry into her unspoken story through any deductive intuition on his part brought alive through associations rekindled between Sela and her childhood home's lush world, with the finer details carefully hidden away in places only she could share if willed to do so without proper cause as a slip of misspoken words or a careless revelation during an unguarded moment. Generally, Sela wasn't prone to sharing details of herself, at least not since she gained the invested experience enough to better appreciate the benefits of self-control by keeping "my shit to myself," even with Josh with the fullest comprehension of chronological transitions both past and future and the values in her further silence.

She often felt the urge to confess to somebody, even a stranger or a dying bed to whisper her secrets to the occupant before departing, and thereby trick as wisdom her stealthy words to the otherworld, though "it isn't my confession to tell," later burning the small paper from the end of her cigarette until it was a charred fleck between her distressed, chafing fingers as she let it loose to the wind for the flexibility to swiftly blow on the sharp burn of her skin.

It didn't seem like her story to confess. Her admittance would sound implicit with culpability by the act of her telling it. Hearing herself relate her story would have made her objectively vulnerable to her own critical inner self helplessly screaming at her physical peripheral to stop the words waved into vibrational exposure to a distrusting outer world beyond her ability to collectively control. It would have involved her, and Josh by the association of her telling it aloud, in something she didn't claim as ownership and which in doing would have been the ruination of her innocence by painfully trying to restrain her distending thoughts over her misspoken misstep and self-blame into some form of workable backtracking or an unavoidable future collusion.

"Of some things, you must never speak, and please be careful with yourself," she once didn't write down, instead letting loose her pen to the wood of the table as she pushed the paper away as a forgotten, unspoken falsehood to better sow through the discipline of her not speaking of it.

She gave him the less significant story of herself, unadventurous in details though extensive enough with the omittance of finer minutiae. There were hints she suspected Josh of hearing in the emotive inflections of her *word-choices* intended as deflection from a truth she naturally found stressful to keep to herself, with the tenuous care she had to take not to reveal the wrong thing, to omit, avoid and overlook during the moments of conversations, challenging her words before speaking them for potential exposure, to not let herself fall into the pitfalls of lies similar to how others kept the secrets of a lifetime of certain prior choices tightly concealed in a tiny box.

Sela knew that not to be able to tell Josh meant the likelihood there would never be anyone to tell it to other than to herself and the winds of her coastline as her sole confidant the same as when she was a child, with the higher chance of inevitable madness the longer she lived with it.

"The thing which must be avoided in life, I mean to try to avoid," she confessed to a note.

"A lot of books," Josh highlighted with genuine amazement for the high volume he saw with a cursory check for genres and names.

"Yeah, Henry liked to read. It's not a collection, more like residue, wasn't much else to do for him, so lucky thing for him I guess."

"Residue?" Josh laughed at the idea of the titles he began to peruse as left-over, and a sad idea to foster.

"Dust. He just liked to read. He didn't like

to get rid of them after he read them even though he never looked at them again, but I think he liked them around for me to have to fountain my interests as I grew up, also with nothing else to do, so lucky for me too. They were always there for me to dig through. I read many of those. He had good taste. Hate to think how I could have been shaped otherwise if his interests had lied elsewhere, with pulp of some kind, imagine romance, or westerns. I would have approached the world differently. Of course, he would have had to be different too, so there's that as well," Sela continued until she felt the realization that she was talking on about nothing at all, caught between two worlds while her normalizing attempts at conversing became emotionally overwrought with a sense of not being alone. She found herself feeling uncomfortable being seen by another so close, as if she were an insect under glass with a huge monster's eye fixedly watching her in isolation.

"What do you think he found in the end from all that dedication to reading?" Josh had the urge to ask from his own self-interest and preoccupied nature with reading, not knowing as a novice due his lesser years the result of an aged expert reader as Henry appeared to have been from a closer view of the room and inspection of the choice of names for the time they were read in the seventies and eighties, and the remoteness of the location in navigating the books there. Josh knew he could spend many years living in the house reading from this room, once a crude study room for Henry, if the chance had been available for him to repeat a life in his own lesser way, but he was only staying a few weeks before getting back to home and work in the city.

He perused the many bookshelves lining two walls, with other books stacked on tables and the floor, finding one entire shelf dedicated to books for children and teens, textbooks, classics and a profoundly serious sampling of world literature and modern tomes shaping the psyche of humanity disheveled across an entire wall in a manner of having been read and cast aside for the next reader to arrive in proper time. The next reader had been Sela as she grew up with her small, limited library of personal choice awaiting her. She had held and slowly turned the pages of many of these books, the oils and sweat from her fingers marking a signature attachment with the paper, the same as Henry and Ruth having each read a particular assortment of the whole collection, with the books taken away, owned during consumption, and returned for the next, future handler.

Josh felt a bit privileged to have seen this aspect of Sela's past as a sighted and rounded explanation of the woman he knew.

He imagined the old man he had seen in one of the few framed pictures of Henry scattered about the house, with long gray hair and wrinkled smile, living his life in the natural setting, walking the beach, with his family, the freedom of leisure with books and a slow fade.

He envisioned Ruth the same during her homeschool teaching with Sela as sole pupil for her attentions, allowing shorter learning days and abundant opportunity for higher learning through the experience of applying the things she found in Ruth's teachings and books with her natural world all around through the sighted practices of play and imaginary games of heroic wonder.

Josh smiled with envy at the image of the old man reading under the sun, on the rocks of the beach or sitting in one of the weather-worn wooden chairs located about the grounds, each carefully placed for vantage, shade, sun's exposure or isolation, and the images of a running Sela as a younger girl similarly charmed and with better context for Josh abetted by his imagination for the woman he knew only for a few years as an adult while staying as guest in the home of her childhood.

"The same as everyone else in unique ways, envisioning it has all been a rolling barbaric challenge regulated by the rules of past persuasion," was the answer she wrote for herself later in the night when alone.

With his presaging nature, the books had been for her protection and prewarning of a world no longer meant to embrace her nature, leaving her vulnerable to its exorbitant influence more than most without proper understanding usually unmasked through the preserving of experience and its summated outcomes as proof of actions to take.

She had read the books and many others in the comfort of an adult future she came to live, and she had found many sources for insight and passion, thinking these minds must provide answers, which they did while seeking the same perplexities she faced and endured as trials through worded penetrations while questing after the same answers with uniquely attached turmoil: by journey as ancient hunters of the reality imposed upon them with depthless neglect and precious guardedness.

She only came to accept later and recently that her quest was the same eternal, riddled quest followed by the reoccurring few bound to it and by whatever impending, pressing and impenetrable urge to compete in gamely compulsion within whichever presented designs had been afforded them as a field upon which to play as ruled temporal contexts of actionable meaning.

The world, if deserving or crossing a threshold of falsehood beyond a tolerance, forced each by appetite to mutually play along as force to an intimate challenge to become prime, storming contenders for nature's pride.

"There is something strange in the pursuit of words, or art of any kind, a sense of being unworthy and privileged through its performance. The feeling can also apply to reading and looking into art for meaning. The pursuit of meaning is a peculiar thing to look for. In the natural world, the exact same pursuit is for survival and improvement, where the species and individuals are the mutual cause and effect of continuance, the art itself roving reality as a fixed, moveable and flexible canvas stretching into all senses of it. Art is reality. True art and truer words work and retexture its malleable surfaces, like it's been skilled and anciently perfected for a relative forever. In comparison, what are our words? What is our art? I think we should be too ashamed to speak, to draw, to play with these toys in our hands we shape and call artful and assume it filled with our self-meaning."

~~

Beyond the familial fantasies of a youthful child, having a child of her own was never a consideration up to that point in her life, and it was difficult for her to convincingly make that choice for another unborn person, knowing as an experience the force of contrast permeating the world in opposition by either gender, or the unsolvable conflicts of paradoxical personalities ceaselessly rehappening. Through another aspect of her awareness, it was also a choice she could have taken away for the true value of its encounter with a natural, celestial world in which the physical world was the regulated one to be braved as a field in endless contest for emotional persistence.

The memories of Sela's mother lied outside the house. They were in the garden as Sela pointed out hidden behind grassy overgrowth, looking closer at scarred wooden stakes and strung wires thinly rusted while still withstanding an elemental, chemical battle with time's disuse.

"I suppose I should clean that up, maybe grow some vegetables for the summer," she included as explanation, "everything I need should be here, in the shed where Ruth left it last," indicating with her pointing finger, alongside the casual use of her mother's given name the same as she had recently used "Henry" a number of times, to the oversized wooden structure with the barred doors and little else showing from behind the grassy, bushy overgrowth with no one around to push it back, similar to the rest of the landscape outside the house overgrown with natural leafy shag. "The keys should be hanging inside on the wall-pegs behind the door. I'll look when I go in."

"I can help you with that while I'm here.

Clear some of this back. Did Ruth garden? Grow things?" It was one of the few questions he had ever asked about Sela's mother, previously waiting for her to bring her up until she didn't offer anything of detail, and he was compelled to be prudent in asking as curiosity he couldn't resist any longer in support of a sympathetic custom.

"Yes, we ate from the foods she picked and grew. She was personally close to nature by the time I knew her. She admired this place she was able to live in, praising it by pointing it out to me in microscopic details I can recall sounding poetic through her voice and the way with her words. She was always growing, pickling, cooking, and sealing," Sela freshly replied with a first hint of excitement. "I can see her in that chair over there under the sun cleaning and trimming her freshly picked vegetables from her woven, dirty wicker basket, or walking to the creek to wash the dirt off, crouched, leaning forward dunking the basket and washing her hands while I lingered around her. The ends of her skirt would be soiled with dirt and water. The little birds would flitter about enjoying her companionship. Only occasionally, whether by secret marker or sympathy, would she feed them a few seeds, disdainfully tossing them to the ground like coins ringing the concrete for a beggar. At the same time, she would sit back and watch them pick at the seeds like her sympathy was a scented affection they eagerly shared to consume," as Sela stopped with an encouraging smile, having already said more than she had expected to as an avoidance of an emotional state distracting her while she felt the urgency to regain her confidence enough to stay focused.

She realized she had been talking as if no one were there listening while she spoke aloud to herself, and it was truly her memories to have been vocalized aloud absent her attention to the moment with Josh, affronted suddenly to stop as the awareness of an imposed rudeness to reiterate memories unrelated to someone else present with her and briefly forgotten.

"Thinking too much of written words can make you careless with vocal conversations," she reminded herself again.

Sela had already lived the loss of her parents during an earlier time here and suffered it well enough then to last as a lifetime, aching mark.

This time, her return home had a different reason to fulfill, and a different connotation of *mark*.

By Sela's design of daily planning, having been keeping busy around the home and forested beachscape during the time back with Josh as companionship, they decided a few days before he was due to leave to take a ride to a scenic local sight Sela wanted him to see before leaving or he would "end up seeing nothing at all," promising a surprising location or two he should enjoy for the "nature of it," or just a day trip around the area she had been previously reluctant to show him, making excuses of other things to do around the house, avoiding the rainy days, while scheming the twofold intention of concealing from the locality her newly arrived presence back at the house with her beachscape world to emotionally reclaim as hers.

It was to protect Josh from local exposure and ready herself for the job ahead of her, starting a few mornings later when she expected to ride him off the two-hour drive each way to the nearest town with a car rental, and from there he was to continue his journey home.

In the used, all-wheel hatchback she bought for cheap before they left to cover the distance to the coast, as well as intended for herself in case of potential emergency requirement and for the odd supply runs during the summer months ahead, they leisurely traveled the coast for an hour until Sela cautioned Josh to turn off and follow along a graveled, pocked road twisting its way through the lush, unkept forest.

After twenty minutes of sharp turns trailed through untouched old growth, they came upon a circular parking area just adjacent the road, marked by the short metal railing with an opening for the pebbled path leading to a small beach inlet sniffed before sighted as they walked closer.

Early afternoon, there were four other vehicles distributed about the lot when they parked the car, for the spot was a local favorite attraction for walks and people to bring dogs or to laze on the rocks, though there weren't a lot of locals or tourists to enjoy it off the beaten track and situated as a secret ending to a lost road.

The pathway weaved through bushes with high grasses interspersed with occasional virgin blooms of spring wildflowers. Moving over a small hillock blocking the view, they descended onto a new beachscape blocked by cliff faces a short distance either way and a far waterline revealing the sandy underbelly of the shore during low tide. An inlet off the ocean, scanning the waters revealed surrounding forests in the distance.

"I made sure when we got here when it was low tide," exposing a clandestine motive, "as you can see."

Under the cliffs, during the low tide, monstrous greyish and rust-colored boulders were exposed otherwise unobservable when the tide was high.

"The tides can quickly rush in when it comes. You wouldn't want to get caught hopping boulders trying to outrace an approaching wave, but it's a number of hours away yet, so we can safely go out."

Stepping onto the finely pebbled beach,

there were a few small groups of people gathered one way further down to the right under the hardened cliff face, and a man strolling the water's edge over the puddled sandy bars exposed and gleaming under the sun, playing with his mixed Labrador with a large stick too big which etched a mark in the sand with its relentless drag as the dog wasn't going to give it up, lifting its head to raise it up only to have gravity drag it back down like a stone of Sisyphus.

They laughed at the persistent tendency of pooch humor repeating itself as they tended to do together at the sight of dogs.

"Don't you love a dog's sense of humor?"

"I know. You must have come here as a child?"

"Yes, sometimes they brought me here, and Henry would take me out to there so we could sit and look back from atop a big rock at the water's edge, just to turn and look back."

Reaching the water's edge, the ocean's waters, standing stop a large circular rock, one of many stretching a far distance back to the shrunken beach and the raised, viewable rocky cliffs with a surprising, towering lighthouse atop unseen from the beach.

As with the sight of any lighthouse, there is the expectation of an unlivable, disused symbol of a former time auraed from the antiquated beacon as a highest point once warning to seafarers approaching from the ocean the other side of the inlet beyond.

"Such crude warning systems, but they worked and traversed time," Josh interjected.

"Yes, through multiple world conflicts they stood firm. I always loved the view when we got here and finally looked back which I'd avoid doing until we reached this spot, the whole thing with a shrunken illusion of distance making it look so far away. Doesn't it make you feel huge? Like a giant, at least as a kid it did."

"Yeah, it does. As an adult too."

As usual on his journeys with Sela, she brought into his life the most adventurous sights he might not have found otherwise and told her so to which she kindly smiled, not furthering the conversation by telling him he was the only one she shared such sights.

"I would be standing here alone if you didn't choose to join me, come with me when I ask, travel with me even for reasons wholly my own," she rethought.

Skimming down the side of the boulder he had stood on alone, he leapt to hers to stand together.

"Takes some practice but gets easier, you

did this as a kid?"

"Like you said, it gets easier with practice. Ruth hated it, but Henry showed me to take care and stay focused, like not looking back until the end, a kind of discipline better for a kid to learn to feel and not ignore as the useful thrill of emotion controlled in action between the girl and the risky rocks."

"Risk enhances the discipline," Josh intuited, "especially when you would have to live with it either way for you to learn it."

"True, Henry did take an elevated risk for me, to elevate my confidence then and now."

"I suppose you're lucky. To learn as most kids would never get the chance, with risks."

~~

Inevitably, with the persuasion of time, they began to head back, urged by the tepid question from Josh, "when exactly is the tide due back?"

With the practice of getting out to the water's edge behind them, the return trip, keeping balance and footing while leaping the large, sun-exposed rocks with pock-marked exteriors in which collected tiny, pooled versions of the ocean waters with assorted kelpy and shelled remnants clinging to the hot surface in hopes of a refreshing tidal shift, was faster.

As Josh and Sela followed a separate route of walking stones, they naturally began to race in competition near the end until Sela appeared first onto the pebbled beach hopping from the last rock like a gymnast making her landing to finish a perfect performance, raising her arms straight above, only briefly so as not to regret her enthusiasm as overexcited during inevitable hind-sighted moments, as a disciplined protection of her future from her present interactions in situations.

She wildly, excitedly smiled at the day's peculiarity.

"It must look totally different during high tide," Josh envisioned, "does the water completely conceal the rocks?"

"You know," Sela admitted, "I always assumed it, but I've never been here during high tide, they always made sure it was during low tide when we came. I can't remember to see it with high tide to tell you."

There was the unmentioned visit with Cheryl during the summer she stayed two weeks at the house as a short visit after their graduation three years earlier, and a seeming beginning or starting point to Sela's resulting escape and cautious return then with Josh, if one needed to be pinpointed as defining an aged, reoccurring conflict, but it was low tide then too when they had hopped the rocks, as a freed, carefree summer laugh, to the water's edge for the view back at the rocky cliffs with a lighthouse atop.

Standing out on the farthest rocks at low tide, with the wide distance between herself and the shore, it felt like treading water in the ocean depth, and Sela embraced the space and greater distance from everyone else as pleasingly familiar to her while overwhelming for others as an undying, imprisoning emptiness and solitude not worth living.

A lingering sense of wounding humiliation haunted her as a mocking reflection as real as her recently recalled imagination's openness to resentment, as much as she tried to make it work while going to school and working in the city.

Especially regretfully resentful then was the fact of her lack of choice resulting in her cowardly retreat from here when she had fled three years ago, only to come back much later with ample enough bravery.

"You had no choice except to leave," she comforted herself as reminder. She knew her excuse only applied to her present state then, for only in hindsight were there alternatives, though each were fraught by limited justifications for seamless confidence of success.

It was normal to support the silence, the same as the emptiness, unlike living in the city with its loud fullness, where "you must be secretive to avoid discomfort in overtly sensitive others not used to the stillness."

In nature, she found the unrelenting sounds of the otherwise silent existence unheeded by impassioned defenses of renunciation.

By population size, it was only a village with a few adjacent side streets off a main road with scarce local shops, but there was a fruit stand, so they pulled off the road at Josh's suggestion on the way back home.

He picked out cherries and tiny apricots recently plucked from a local greenhouse orchard.

The old woman working the till, only recognized by Sela as they placed the fruit down, was the same woman working there over the span of all the years as a youth whenever she would stop at the stand to buy fruit with Ruth. The woman, whose name Sela couldn't recall if she ever knew it, comfortably approached her with a reaching hand and touch of Sela's arm, telling her of the long time since she last saw Sela, asking how she was, offering sorrow for her parents, and with fairness how she'd grown to be so beautiful a woman, to which Josh smiled and agreed knowing his friend's easy modesty.

Part of not taking Josh to view the sights of the area sooner was her concealment of her past, her humiliation at not being expectantly familiarized with the local people of the environment she grew up in, everywhere revealing a friendlessness and amiable distance on her part, and shameful of a quiet child still inside her pressing the folds of her regrets over the alleged loss of chances to further and better experiences.

"There was never much there for you," she admitted to herself, "though not to mean that there's nothing there to find without you."

She knew from being recognized by the woman; her ready presence was no longer locally unseen. In fact, soon everyone would know even if most wouldn't have reason to care other than Sela being the daughter of Ruth and Henry whom none really knew too well other than being amiable and reclusive.

"There is good and evil because the ideas exist and there are those willing or compelled to pick a side," the words of Henry resounded in her head in as clear a raspy voice as when he first spoke the words to her as prewarning, "and sometimes the world is such that you have to fully embrace the choice made, usually by the unkindness of others."

He had kindly used the word "*unkindness*" with dire-rooted nuance, "even to kill to protect your own if it's forced upon you. Make sure you pick the side that's you, and practice it, there is no middle path to follow," he prophetically finished with a similar sounding inflection of "*forced*" even if differently connotated.

"If it comes to it, be careful of the ones to try to stop you," as words recalled with deeper overtones later as an adult, without proper relevance as a secluded child living in an unsuspectingly disordered world.

There was someone somewhere, as she was formally, intuitively, and recently acutely aware, alert to her. Someone to have made an intimidating maneuver directed at her intimation of fear. Someone believed to know of her life and her history connected to the house and beach. A stranger was focused with suspicious intent upon her, for her discomfort and the helpless humiliation of her forced interest in an alleged, faceless and ghostly figure stalking her whereabouts while successfully amplifying her emotional sensitivities beyond her willingness to continue in any unchallenged way, to not be preyed upon as if she were nothing more than a victim for another's amusement, "again." It newly absorbed her concentration with its disruption to her better focus upon a preferably self-determining future.

"Robbing me of an open, carefree present and predictable future," through an unfinished connection in her past.

The same as with the presence of the playful outsider she found in nature as a child befriended through her active imagination, now as an adult she sensed the same presence in a shadowed stranger with a different resolve unsolicited by any except an ignoble natural world.

Later, over prior years, during her walks at night in the city, she had begun to stalk the stalkers, sometimes straight to their dens, hovering outside, watching for the lights to go out. She considered herself practicing their world to outwit it through heeding the opinions of weakness, scouting the vulnerabilities and bounds of a roving, faceless foe she couldn't properly disarm or be rid of for herself and the world fast enough.

She practiced finding the predators, being drawn to them, and knowing before they did of her presence in the camouflaged disguise of "just another roaming sheep gone astray."

On a dark night, she had hidden in the trees after sliding off the narrow path she had been following for its promise of brief solitude. It was autumn with no insects and the underbrush was flattened with a rusty crunch audible walking through it.

The quiet of her lingering aloneness had disturbed a near audible vibration alerting her to something else of big scale close by. If she had continued her forward path, rather than deviate as she did instead into the trees, like any doe too close to a leopard's pounce, she would have found out of the other through a dissimilar abuse of her senses.

An unseen, corrupted caricature of predatory nature had already arrived and slithered into the trees further ahead of her. She didn't want to come out of her hiding spot by making a sound, though she realized her being there should already be known.

They lingered in the aftermaths of history, even when there was doubt, awaiting the next crystalizing courage to rise as the waves of the next destruction, and the organized enablers of villains. There was no escaping them, with an endless streak of wars fought to suppress them, but they always survive to persist by her feminine sympathy to name her own blame as one of many blames, making of her higher gifts instead her vulnerability before the celestial beast obstructing her otherwise enthusiastic serenity.

For long moments which stayed motionless, she pondered her power to act, her senses alerted and fixed upon the unseen, merely felt stalker once it mistakenly sounded its tread, like two competing predators locked in staring bluff.

She stopped it by turning and walking away, back in the direction of the path and the safer glow of the city, culpably knowing she had walked that way too much before at too consistently a time during the night. She needed to stagger her times better, experiment with new paths, and not be so predictable.

With the next resounding treading through the leaves behind her, Sela bolted towards the lights of the city, her ears echoing with the scrunching sounds of the crusted leaves barely audible above her pulsing blood; and briefly, the overlapping sound of similar crushing steps running from behind her before they begin to fade as the bulky salivating leopard she glimpsed just once in the shape of a man surrendered the pursuit of its doe as lost.

The doe, with fleeting victory bouncing in leaps from the trees onto the surface of glowing, manicured grasses with an analogously jumping rhythm in her heart, returned to her apartment, tearful and shaken behind a locked door. She realized she had to confront other identities too or be its victim the same as countless, endless others throughout history, for there was no free pass as she concluded then while still in her second year of school long ago one night afraid and alone, with a close call she was cravenly forced to leave in wait for a future reoccurrence to find without her; for the thrill of one of reality's perpetrating pillagers thriving in an environment without the awarenesses she possessed of a natural world beyond her capacity to overlook, as mockingly happy, blissful or arrogantly self-contended persons, with just deceitfulness and possessed of the will to take valued pride in such a dirty victory in secret imitation without the pure predatory impulses mentored by the living opinions of nature.

Looking at herself in the bathroom, she clearly saw the truth of her position in her eyes, and the wrong face to wear as helplessly as she wore it then.

Amazingly, later in bed, she recalled she had been uneasy, emotional, and revengeful, but not fearful.

She would have preferred then to be the predator, to lay in wait for her pseudo-counterpart, enacting an opposing justice, proving the truer prey under the fitting veil of nature's delicate balancing act.

To become that person would be to fully overcome herself through the muffling of her pride in favor of a torturous emptiness and a thundering silence to endure reality as an intimate asylum instead.

Then, it was too soon in her youth to properly sight, only to run from with the gifting learnedness of the prey.

CHAPTER 5: WALKING ON STONES

The raw chafing of the stones pressing beneath footsteps soothes her vein through an immersive reoccurrence she controls as a relaxing, poised focus upon her buoyant passage, with each measured step barely singular from the preceding steps and the steps she has further to come. With each next step, the old sequence resurfaces to repeat again, so long as she stays sensitive to it, like staring at an elementary particle to keep it still and material. In this way, her innermost echoes calmly distend to match the distracting pace of the scuffing sounds in relation to the setting she no longer sees, absorbing the waves of light emanating just for her view from the heated stones, the subtle vibrations of sound mimicking the rhythm of music, and the savoring hint of briny air.

For long spans of time, she could measure and hold the constant moment travelling with and alongside her in flawless synchronization. She had done this as a child and mimicked herself at that age now nearly twenty years later transfixed by the same sharing memory bonded by past and present trying to sustain a unifying perfection through her repeating actions, a timeless merging between herself and the ageless world as a wholeness occurring around her without past, present or future, happening in the wind and the light, in the flowing waters and stubborn trees, in the sand, pebbles and stones, and the force of her comixing, intrusive wandering.

This time, walking the stones as an experienced adult, she is overcome by a seriousness in her bonding meditation not available to the girl as further identity with her virgin memories. It is easier looking back into her past to the girl than the girl could hope to accurately envision her future as Sela now through any honest vigor of her imagination, giving her a sense of sympathy for the naive enthusiasm of the younger version for her blindness to invasive influences to come into her life as an unsought seepage from another world she could only understand with the provisioned time to fathom it better, a luxury not gifted to the newly born but earned through an allotted time to further practice to compete in the contests of real-life arenas.

"The world must be challenged against its rudeness of biased insights, rather than an idea of an unheeded sense unacted upon, nothing more," she had carelessly written, hoping something more of it would come to her later.

In the house, she keeps the pen and paper in one place, Henry's desk, so it doesn't get scattered and lost. Nothing of it leaves his room, the one place it belongs as nowhere else in the world.

The younger girl could barely discern the maturity of the woman as a suggestion to her observations and further senses of the world's goings-on, transfixed in her attentions, fascinations, and keenly to an anticipating nature through its daily transference she would only later learn to be the addictive influences of energies to which all nature cohesively besought for a fresh, soothing fix.

Once sated, energized and freed by the refreshing vigor of its jolting, flowing junk, when the addict was satisfied and withdrawn from hungering urges, with the blood relaxed and contented, it roved as a force of the cosmos with the unyielding strength of vision and powerful insights of a guru manipulator of the loftier scaling dimensionalities of reality, a hidden, ghostly communicator in plain sight, untamed, wild and keen to be drawn awestruck by a rare provoking spirit to spellbind its otherwise unbiased, inattentive curiosity.

The girl found and gave her trust as a witness to this other world of reality by her demeanor she now appears fated to find since it found her as a wistful, wily child in her awkward imaginings of reality. To the fantasies of the child, reality was not a stranger but a watchful actor of the same glowing, dusted world as her.

The entirety of the vision of humanity enacting its enlightened fantasy had hardly been hinted to her then, making her freed and slowly, growingly fettered by its incarceration upon her as an experiencing child; yet, without knowing the contrast she knows now as an adult with more experience of the dissimilarity, she would have been expected to be left limited in her appreciation and the current keenness of her attention to it now and into the future with greater power of will for its loss of practice and compounded diminishment.

"Who could I be now instead?" She dreads to think of an answer as a wasted expense upon her prompt predictabilities better focused elsewhere with the gladness of dismissal for what she views in the world as the havens of alternatives.

Even as a child, she was transfixed by an imaginary secret gaze slowing drawing its awareness to herself identical to her inner-staring focus upon it, spotting the patterns of whispered utterance exuded like a seepage through a detection of its coordinating movements in relationship to her active choices.

She recognizes the drifting child visibly in the concealed cues of her beachfront world beyond herself in this instant of time and with her gifted control of the moment, as if the moment now were the moment then, with the same sounding meandering of winds and moist air teaching her mutually during her shared solicitudes, encouraging further desires for recurring aloneness to feel its presence and hear the simple words of existence as a vocalized, murmuring suggestion in her imaginings of a different world of spiritual substance veiled behind the surfaces of things, within the densities of stone and bark, in the recurring waves from the ocean whispering the same now as then and a million or billion years ago, endlessly in different spaces just like her beach "bending and flipping reality until you come to finally believe you hear the light and see the sounds interchangeably focused inside you as the sole interpretation defining the universe in inflating scales of blurring coordination."

It was a game in a child's mind to peer behind the moveable glaze, beyond the physical to the enacting disturbances of the real world instructing it, the speaking appendages animating the playful string-puppets afforded of reality, inclusive of herself emerging into a recollecting identity as the game evolved into an awakening adulthood of negotiated experiences with its increasing detachment from the younger child within the adult woman as the breakage from a cocoon, a new second skin with the old left behind like a snake's to wither with the dust and the rocks of eternity.

With the further rhythming coincidence of overlapping temporal occurrences, she sees the child was fearless and controlled in her secret association with her animated, luring, friend-like stranger of nature. The sole distinction between the child then playing with her imagination as the method of finding herself and the adult now as somehow found is merely the difference of a followed, involved and practiced skill and its cohesive learning, between the natured young girl and pronounced urban woman, and she has been fittingly doused by both conjecting waves of reality as she hastens upon the merging fertile ground of the proffered mixture besmirching upon her as sole conflicting endpoints to unravel for solutions masquerading as meaningful answers, blending her life into an inner world of limiting, fixed hesitations from which she must feast her attentive sustenance as if a choice of truth, rather than an addict of reality like all the rest of it.

She envisions ahead as well to the older woman she will become in the future looking back at herself now reflecting in the colored stones at her childhood image as if a wandering traveler after the wordless solution to an unsolved ancient mystery, a worn away fossil of herself from a distant, rekindling time due a prior life. In this instant, she feels the obligation she owes both the child left behind and the impending old woman as a unifying journey through an experience of reality, as a face of the universe making of her a context, a series of self-choices for overall distending betterment or impoverishment, as an attempting answer and a communication of whispering, coinciding and contesting rapports as dialogue through the happenings of reality for a lack of anything more substantial to affix for support in an otherwise emptiness.

Looking down at the approaching stones deciding her path identical in sight as the ones before, she gleams at the focused young girl intently listening to the squashing grind beneath her footsteps, the rounded stones like soft, wet, sandy ground giving under her lightly weighted pressure steadily pounding a malleable, releasing landscape with her insignificant presence as a new shaping of the universe glued to her changing movements within it.

She clearly remembers the girl walking by herself on the isolated beach as if the two moments were tightly pressed and overlapping as a cooccurrence, since her memories are often fixed and presently enthralled, renewed again by the pleasing celebration cued into being by her return to this beach; but that girl was not as able to look forward to the woman she becomes mimicking her absorbed playfulness in her own confidently misplaced future, as a lesson to heed now.

The salted, breezing air provokes within her an exciting, cleansing sympathy for the child making as a distraction of the moment a plaything of the entire world of appearance and surfacing actions as if belonging to her alone.

Stopping to look about, scanning the wind-slanted tree line artfully marking the beach's chiseled withdrawal, to any observing animal eyes hidden inside perked to attention and peeking at her strange, isolated presence, and other than being herself and not another person instead, she now knows by her return that as a human being she is meant as an exiled stranger from this natural world accorded an ancient, pagan choice and the self-imposition of her species into the mystical realms of an iconic world imposed upon the natural mysticism of an eternity to come before it.

She stands as the current representation, the transformed victim of that long-ago spiritual breakage into the confounding milieus of idealistic caricaturized fates as the emblems of higher truths.

She is persuasively overcome by the impression of the unsuspecting child fearlessly standing and singly playing near the ocean's edge, on the threshold between two wild, sanctioning worlds of cunning engagement on either side of her, one in the waters farther from her reach and the other closely forested and wildly confined. She looks now, fearful solely for the faded child, the staring waywardness of impassioned, hungered animals there then the same as undoubtedly now, buried beyond the rhythmically counting shore, stony beach and soft driftwood trunks, within the forests and hills awaiting the skilled chances of coinciding happenstances fueling a natural realm's vitality in the captivating contest of worldly furtherance.

An obvious, easy mark in the ogling or predatory eyes of some transitory assortment of avian, feline or canine genus assimilated to the area, her small, isolated child-self fixated upon the pattern of her steps should have been overwhelmed with the sense of her vulnerable dignity, eying herself only now with adult eyes as "a slowly walking meal," but the child she images was forever fearless in her endeavors. There was barely a sense of risk, and an unafraid trust in her detachment from a world of reciprocally uncertain dangers and its habituated, predatory bent of nature. Nature recognized the predator not the prey in the stature of the girl while barely capable with her skills.

"If you can imagine it, I read somewhere Orcas have never killed a human being in the wild," she had recounted to Josh before further philosophizing it, "it seems impossible to fathom, from all the possible encounters and chances, of what has mostly been perceived as a big, aimless fish, but doesn't it make it sound as if we are excluded, invisible, shunned as an exile cast from that world of seriousness. As if nature compassionately determined not to admit the human being any longer among itself, at least in the eyes of the Orcas as protest. A way of communicating we haven't yet heard this long in the future. That they made this choice and recognition long ago, anciently even, before we had the will to make the distinctive association we can only barely make now in hindsight, for it is never foresight with us, only with the Orcas, the Oracles of the Sea when it comes to seeing our true worth."

"Other animals kill us, sharks, snakes, crocodiles."

"Yes, but perhaps not so much the highly honorable or genetically predisposed ones."

"Genetically predisposed, with what?"

"I don't know, maybe an empathic sense of ironic embarrassment. I can imagine we might appear intolerably pubescent to more than just a few of ourselves as a context within the universe, and the rest of the animal world too sighted enough to see or close enough to come across our paths. I would like to hope so anyway."

"I don't know, we must be as least worth eating, we can't be shunned that far that we can't even be eaten," Josh enthused, as they walked the beach together before he left.

"Personal vengeance taught by experience to individual members of higher acting animals maybe, we might still be worth that, for the few, and there are plenty of humans ready and eager to mockingly poke a stick or throw a rock at that imbalance of fairness, much like bullying."

At least, it roused a laugh together with its comforted kindness to nature's paleness.

Now, as an adult, she walks and stands on these same stones as the girl of her youth, and with no physical harm done, no animal attack from the trees or the oceans, and no permanently painful memories caused by the world of nature she looked for and willfully found as a nurturing, faithful companion to herself as an obscure child, except within the confused psyche of the adult woman in confrontation with another, abstracting reality in opposition.

Standing before the trees now as then, she has lost something as subjective revision during the time away from here. Living within a world of people, alone in believing this world she saw in her youth to be vibrant and full of insightful vigor rather than empty of such imaginative value. The personality the child found secretly protruding from flowing occurrences as they related to her, if not visible to others as she only really learns later with a sincerity confusing her integration in the unban world, believing this perception to be ordinarily possessed within the human realm as an exclusive mastery of the universe temporally occurring; instead, she discovered "a place of worsening bewilderment all around her transfixed upon an ever-spiraling dissolution of preconceived wonderlands."

Everything humanity touches as a measure of itself continues the evolution of approaching its endgame without the sightedness she found and continues to further look for from the ancient world viewable in the present world.

Most of a small part of all existence is predatory, as this world exemplifies, to which she gifts herself omitted as concerns nature intimating her as either predator or prey in her private relationship with the natural world as a roving trick she confidently seizes for the protection of its blending oversight.

From a beginning, she watchfully associated with this closed world as an expectation of a welcoming nature instilled as a bonded lifeblood through a relating affixation with the child of her youth, rather than the distinction of merely being born a human being of marked spiritual size against the otherwise immensely starry nights of a boundless universe.

As a younger adult, thoughtless of her childhood wonderment, she had left this forgotten world to have forgiven her as an individual contrary to most of the rest of her kind in charm, unbeknownst to the rooted notice of Sela at the time.

Now, a reclaiming Sela pauses in quiet, greeting homecoming atop the stones of her beach, a maturing predator proudly standing strongly prime before the trees, the waters behind her with the winds at her back blowing her hair across her face like the strings of a flitting, eroded time besieged to challenge the fraying eternities overwhelming it, as the infinite moments stretching forever become too much for time to any longer curtail.

As a defenseless object of nature, she should have been perceived an easy prey, but she wasn't a prey or seen as one within this mystical reality. The animals, the trees and waters, the long-living atmosphere of this natural facet of hidden existence, each and collectively accepted the distinction of her daring remoteness and let her be as a moveable spirit, viewed as iconic in her timeless singleness as a wandering child sighted in the completeness of her lifetime beaming through her fluttered, youthful reflection in its pagan eyes, rather than as a moment in time coincidently, incidentally and tactlessly chanced for her to become instead a lively, meaty, slow object hungrily torn to bony shreds and thirstily bled as fitting to her naïve, defenseless fragility as a more appropriate, alternate fate.

There is a different fitness Sela possesses, marked by the careful eyes and pinpointing senses of nature during those childish quests. As an adult, she has an obligation to the child and the nurturing generosity which allows her susceptible spirit to continue to play and grow through her coincidental, driven encounters, much as sensory-channeled instructions tricking into collective articulation for the mind its outer reality with the full, faithful trust of its appearances, textures, scents, hints and wordless spirits, and without any urge to dismiss, misuse or conquer it.

"There are invulnerable spirits that bite," Ruth had told her as a warning for a child to heed.

~~

As a practice of mounting recurrence, preemptive emotive burdens would intermittently begin to rouse and fantastically surge through her body as coarse blood streaming through barbed veins, a dragging new discomfort pricking her sensitivities, forcing skillful control of her alertness, her calm composure, with a shifting gamut of frequently pounding feelings she has previously familiarized as a normal inner experience of the world within her willpower to undergo in anticipation, as a vulnerable flaw of her character to better overcome by misrepresenting it to all others except to herself and any mutual stranger with the sighting integrity to actually perceive her the same, though she can't say with full confidence she has ever met that person or ever would meet him, her or them as an intimacy in the future to follow.

This reoccurring affection questing for the

missing aspect of social interactions stays with her, deciding her indecisions, and misplacing her self-controls. With an emotive attunement for the sensations of existence itself, rather than the senses of her body alone in isolation, as an affecting attachment to the beliefs she musters as a near constancy of sensory suggestion the more experienced she becomes as a participating inhabitant of the world, she is prone to this facet of reality, dissimilar to all others unless there exists a conspiratorially well-kept secret excluding her as an unsuspecting victim or mark from everyone else, an obviously paranoid conduit of orbiting irrationality to admit rather than dismiss as a dangerously delusional path to traverse proudly alone.

In this way, to salvage an identity, she must admit the alternative to herself, confidently viewing her presence as somehow beyond the paled light of otherwise diminishing awarenesses looked for and found as best effort before her, lasting for eons of endlessness bringing her here to freely consider herself "*perhaps*" to be autonomous.

"Once we arrive here, born to emotively learn in thought this reality as fit, the eternal vainly stills for us to see its riddled, colored agony of endurance, a meticulously crafted thing contrary to an otherwise unheard hollowness," she had wanted to speak with lofty words to Josh sitting on the rocks of the beach during a warm evening, but instead for comfort, "a beautiful evening, isn't it?"

"It is. It really is," replied a mutually ruminant Josh with the abrupt descent of night's darkness soon after accompanying them on the walk back to the house.

She thinks of herself as "hyper-emotional," and laughs when she says it aloud with no one else there, until she realizes she is confusedly absorbing the funereal, human-influenced world around her instead as an imitating reflection of her interpretation of herself in confusion.

Sometimes, when it occurs as a prolonging load she quietly carries around as her burden to convey to keep her identity to herself at least, seeking self-distraction from its enablement inside her until inevitably days would arrive when her muscles and bones ached from the moment she awoke, a reply forcing her to reflect and regain control of herself by whatever means to alleviate the coaxing physical pressure on her body by the stress of her emotions.

"Too many lose connection with the child of their youth, through some form of self-serving brutality, they must live an adulthood contending with the impression of an infancy lost to unsolicited associations.

"This callused world of fantasy and circus. With me, I find there are times I'm alert in the moment, and other times when I'm there in the same way, but also not there. There's a difference in some situations and others, a difference of coping, of a redirecting handling of the complexed moment which should otherwise occur the same, with the same emotive response except for the incomprehensible change fixating my attentions during heightened observations, such as larger, unfocussed crowds or its anticipation of interactions.

"Yet the real world seems intent on prodding and testing us as individuals and as a species with moral labyrinths we must traverse to a fitting end; a feat it doesn't take a direct contact with nature to occur the same in the city as the mountain, even for the victimized role of prey as a fitness of endgame survivals.

"Except, the moral labyrinths have already been solved, finely mapped, and gutted of implications other than as a practical, coaxing ploy of some over others as control. They were proved to be unreal and merely practical," she wrote on a full sheet of paper, late at night and the early hours after Josh went to bed and the wind dancing through the leafy trees outside the open window of the kitchen had exhausted itself.

It feels better to write her thoughts down, the ones prominent to her and the first thoughts with a context originally found in her triangulating milieus, and to then decide whether each is worth overlooking or not with a penchant for keeping. She prefers to look at her thoughts in front of her, to realize her wording justice on paper held between her fingers, with the light absorbed by her eyes appraising the words in combination, and thereby entering the translating ideas back into her mind as a new thought through the act of rereading rather than roving the infinities of forgetfulness in her mind, as if etched in wood as the unfounded, symbolic meaning of eternity.

She adds this practicing routine even though the worded thoughts, pinpointing with finer details her identity with the world, were usually obscurer than the original source of context snatched from a reality of illustrative experiences more selective to her.

She writes down her thoughts to not forget and find better correlations of reality between them, when she remembers to go back and look to find them scattered about the spaces she privately occupied over years, collected and packed to travel with her, so that her writing often became an extended, redundant form of forgetting her thoughts and littering her world, as little as she could ever forget so easily her more pronounced, emotionally exertive experiences with a similar kindness for her to easily circumvent, unmistakably motivated by her willingness not to forget.

She has come to conclude she has only reality to rely on as support and genuine, trusting companionship. While others looked for fixed, embracing successes of social closeness, the sexual dominance and submissions of conquests, the heights of surrenders, politicized resentments, and the amiability of grouped relationships as source for securer, huddling contentment, she quietly sought the opportunities to find reality and see the personalities of a natural existence as delicate details and surprise.

For Sela, the choice was made once it presented itself as her allotted fate, since it wasn't within her to change for others in an essential way harmful to her primal spiritedness and against proper sense for the sake of conformist illusions of sluggish appeasement prevalent in the forgetful, pen and paperless thoughts and beliefs of others frequenting her life in transitory imitations.

At times, for shortened periods, all her emotions would leave her like running, after many days of clear blue skies, into a sudden rainy downpour soaking her in the early morning, as a freshness restarting a new emotional cycle, while briefly the world clearly appeared purer, and her body toiled with the overdue reviving absence of an emotive response, sometimes leading to her self-pitying her prior inner dramas as irrational, but knowing it wasn't *just* her, if not experienced the same as others, and it would inevitably fade away as a fresh reproach from the regaining, newly empowering emotional state of her body's early learned empathies involving upon her psyche the personal resistance of sensory conflict in the correlating adult.

The longer she stays here over the prior weeks, the more she envisions those rainy downpours as a constancy of earthly cleansing absent the constant reflection of an urban circus influencing her otherwise to think differently.

Meanwhile, the actual days and nights around her coastal home have been mostly warm and clear with intermittent rainy days.

Strangely, when noticeably absent for too long, she would begin to miss her dragging emotive burdens as her strength lost, as the source of her words, wondering if she would ever feel again after its briefest respite, as if she might not genuinely experience again a clearer blue sky, existing without associations and the wily patterns of nature, growingly desperate for a glimmering reappearance of fueling panic further debasing her adrenalized passions.

"The wonder of an emotional respite as a cathartic state is its growing panic the longer it is missed from the habit of everyday, or mere hours as a deeper, fearful walk into an unknown, deserted landscape under starless nights.

"If humanity can be deemed obviously impure by its results as a whole rather than in sympathetic isolations, then the challenge for anything true or real must lie in its resistance or difference to that impurity," she thinks and puts down as the first words in a newly started sketchbook, dulling the prior white page she had earlier admired for long quiet moments with a solicitous, empty stare at its brave attempt at a sustaining flawlessness to her senses and devotion.

Soon after she wrote it, she wondered by her worded blotch on the first page whether she should open and restart a new, clean pad.

~~

Sela has the impression of being stuck in place, pasted inside reality, overwhelmed, tossed about and repeatedly crushed by its weightless, exertive forces of particle illuminations as a hurricane over her oceanic moods.

She has been forced by the experiences of her irrefutable senses to learn the motivations of people's actions have become primarily premised on defeat and denial, and no longer trustable in any context of awareness except for a scattered rare she imagined living elsewhere than she has found in her life, a sampling meant to suffer a lost integrity and to naturally strive against it much like a lifelong, endless war or revolt occurring as the historic countryside of an actively stalking psyche finally living its fullest realization in attunement with its world permitting its resistance to thrive in predatory abundance.

Sela supposes such other spirits must still roam the current world, though she has so far, inclusive of herself with doubts, only been introduced to them through books from the past she has read in which they penetrated inventive, properly skewed versions of a presented reality, thereby revealing different layers of awareness to try as newly angled practice in the real world.

Often, this marginalized resistance as a natural reaction of sensitivities to an environment, coupling with temporal associations difficult to correlate, found its proper outlet through written words, the lines of penciled lead on paper, colors on canvas, or another artful exuberance as surrogate for familiarity with the present state in greater conflict.

She can't keep still for long in her relationships as a disciplined constancy for her coiling emotions to better tame her identity without surrendering the risks of fates through the bonding closeness of another person's emotional state as an influence in her life to fully fathom and embrace, creating in her the vulnerability of a fresh, deeply held risk to her future self still in the long midst of transition.

At this point in her life, at least the prior years of her recent memories, she has deliberately permitted her emotive capacity to move freely within her body like the deluged racing of waters over mountainous landscapes, with ground scarring boulders and thrust aged tree trunks cast about like blades of grass in the wind, enamored by its impressive, raging visuals while not offering it seriousness any longer as a source of individuality arriving as a reflection of the outside world shaping her judgements of herself by a different context discovered in the end not to be much context at all beyond the tidbits of misplaced ideas from a forgotten time.

Instead, her roving, cyclical emotions have become a burden of habit to learn to live with, and to develop differently, without knowing exactly how that difference should be better looked for in her world, her solitary figure as the best possibility for it to be found and occur within the light for her scripted awareness alone, rapt in private theatre in which she plays both spectacle and spectator.

"There is no other partner to find to trust," she had whispered to herself, alone in her apartment before she left the city.

With nature, she could freely sense and interact, but not fully commit or communicate as an adept translator, while with people it was more impossibly distant to reach anyone as equalized entities sharing a closed proximity, apart from a few through her life, such as Josh; and otherwise, ephemeral to her time, with youthful depth of properly flouting experiences accumulating aside risk and the ferocity requested of earned, unvoiced truths.

"With each truth newly plucked, we become prisoner to its peculiar silence, for who would believe the voices of truth? In a different age, the fire, the flog or the asylum," she had laughed as disguised sadness with Josh near a small fire sitting atop the stones under the glowing night sky of her beach. She flung the shrunken joint they had finished in the flames with a contented smile. It was one of his last nights with her before he returned to his home.

The more she interacted with people, the more she became caught in their dramatically violent riptides, as if they keep searching for a proof of something never found, never admitting a true defeat except its gilded surrogate, and each alone in the residue, the consequential implications of that unforgivable ride through history sufferable to those sanely living its approaching conclusion into a forceful asylum equally permissible as birthright and deathbed regret.

With others, it isn't a difference of who she is so much as how she is, illegible, indifferent, mute to the misdirected spectacles over higher integrities as proved lacking in her and abundant in relationships as the relaxations of boredom, a limbering stretch of the soul, where an emphatic love is glorified as the recurrent starting point on the way to learning to become revulsive; and interchangeable identities as newfound sources for endlessly characterized inspirations of self-love and degradation alike as the source for the same unheard meaning.

One night, she laughed with sadness, while Josh was still with her visiting at the house, for there occurred a superb full moon phenomenon viewably stirred over the ocean from their fixed perspective.

Not able to help distancing herself, she left him comfortably sitting by the fire to follow the powerful lure of conjuring light boldly exhibiting for her solitude the rare, precious moment boasted in the charmed, reflective angling of night and day between enormous shapes and her solitary perspective, through the collapsing of vast distances and the impossible trick of light's speed coalescing just for her to be capable, through the primal endurance of countless eons, to view by the illusion of shrunken scale a simple performance of the cosmos extending for the possibility to mirror in nodding coordination her intimate exposure to wonder.

Under the night with its gargantuan illusion of closing intimacy, she braved standing before the universe near the water's edge, the air vibrating with the gusting winds and the audible shuddering of the repeating string of waves sinking just as it touches the bare flesh of her sandaled feet, observing its full bloom glowingly cast over the shore and her radiant shadow as a solitary figure viewing its shimmering, brilliant, and broken pathways skimming the ocean's surface until faded against the distant horizon not dissimilar to her than forever.

The patterned light as she saw standing before its occurrence existed solely for her as a reality. The configured light was only for her intending absorption. There was no one else in the world, in the moment, to experience her worldly universe as it occurred to tantalize her corporeal performance as unifying observer. Without her, the universe she created standing on the beach as witness would not occur, faded into the ethereal backdrop of unrealized fulfillments.

Carried by the soulful thrill of a new spectacle of nature, she sat on a small bed of pebbled sand, meditating her presence within such an ineffable thing placed inside her movement of experience shared through the binding of dimly light with the thick fabric of its surfaced debris patterned into sand, rock, water, moon and sky to join her as participating witness and judge properly contextualized alongside the backdrop of nature as fitting Grand Jury of her peers.

"Remember," she said with tender intimation, as prewarning before his trip back home, "this world *can* become an arena for those that succumb to its physical endowments. It can also be an enthusiasm for those that don't and instead find a less forced and balanced path to wander. This life is a journey to find or become stranded by the cleverly physical world and its many shiny, attractive phenomena. Keep a mindfulness of the surrounding equilibrium vital for the penetrating energies of bodily engagements.

"Not that the physical world must be overlooked or undervalued in its posturing, but clearly sighted for its intended, vibrating waves of coiling realities in association, much like light with the capacities of the mind receiving the impressions to faithfully fathom its spectrum."

"Like light?"

"Sorry, I just meant, I guess, relativity applies to more than just light, but to everyone and everything, and our strangely individuated perspectives of things and ideas of the world. So, we can blame Einstein, at least as the one to find it, which is usually enough to call for blame," she joked.

With some things, as a practice, it is impossible to speak plainly assuming the listener is not suspiciously conniving, and this urgency for subterfuge in everyday encounters led her as habit to undeservedly do it with Josh as well, during times when her emotions required veiling, such as his inevitable departure. It wasn't so much his leaving and her being left behind to fend for herself as she planned by intention but knowing that once he left, she would become refocused on her summer trials ahead of her without the excuse or alternative of retreat.

Her foreseen loneliness came from the vital urgency to experience the time ahead alone, to face her unseen fears and keep to herself the eternal secret between herself and the eyes of nature as sole witness, each in confident tandem predicting her survival.

"There is plenty of cleverness to be found in this world, but it must abide by the symmetrical rules of the universe. For this reason, it is best to keep such focus as its seeker of wonder rather than its perpetrator of survived bewilderment along with the bulk of human experiences without leaving any redeeming mark upon the context of the universe yourself," Josh had written with prolonged, kinder words on a note left behind for her to find after he was gone.

~~

There is no expectation her return home will go unnoticed. In fact, she watches carefully for the whispering signs around her, waiting for the time to be hers. She isn't returning to anyone as a reunion in coming back to her home, as shameless as she feels now for having been compelled to leave, but the simple fact of her presence should reignite small embers of curiosity among the locality of strangers casually committed to inclusive, oozingly mindful impositions and diffuse, gossiping snoopiness. Luckily, the formerly boarded-up house is far from any beaten track and her being here will go unseen except by the few as an acceptable risk to chance.

As a preference which extended to Sela during her childhood by association of mutual adoption into an improvised family, Ruth and Henry were solitary and not well-known during the years they lived here.

The house is remote as a choice of location the same as they were as a couple.

With a sunny afternoon, approaching the chair in which she likes to sit near a bed of spring wildflowers, an array of bees surprises her rising from the innards, buzzing and hovering by the hundreds as a single co-acting, interacting entity confronting her face to face like a set of staring eyes. Stopping, the conflagration makes her smile in imitation, and as counter-mimic the buzzing begins to recede in conformation to her rise of enthusiasm.

Slowly, with steady movements, she slides to the chair and sits down with her glass mug in hand, allowing the bees as a throng to settle back and resubmerge into a collective slouch, while the buzzing goes quiet in coordination with her stillness once again, and the spooked, broadened entity descends back to its secret pleasures spoilt by the sweet wildflowers and the release of an intimidating posture meant to guard the covetous, indulgent dependence of a scavenger.

She sets the mug filled with tea on the chair's arm, a closed book on her lap, admiring the quiet interrupted only by the fond caw from a passing crow and the swift frenzy from the synchronized flapping of a band of small birds suddenly appearing with discreet excitement as they closely bypass her sitting in the chair to rapidly land in a nearby bush, coyly stare at her, then just as quick shyly take flight in unison again, having shared enough with her from the hurried perspective of time they consider tangible.

"In this world," she had written, "it can be best to encourage others to underestimate you."

The same as with a whale pulsing through water, or a gull floating a cut through the air, each enacted as a collective of surfaces layered to maneuver in a landscape of myriad such collected and dispersed surfaces, riding the currents and waves of this forceful layering of surfaced actuality.

A world in its unseen minuteness to its celestial artworks to be sketched by finite surfaces of which she is a mere single collective of existence attuned to a shorted, mirrored natural world, otherwise completely insignificant and meaningless to the universe except through the magnitude of her perceiving it in communication with her mute, associating awarenesses of it as a reacting, living world worth her consideration and sighted sympathy for what it otherwise missed for so long from the multitudes of others "ruthless to its sights," she alleges solely by her intimate vision of it through her remote, untranslatable experiences of a younger age.

"In other ages, the banishment of sightedness thrived vast industries of belief acting in uncoordinated effort against its unfair discipline as an enemy worthy of 'no mercy' as a best fit," she thinks for it would be illegible on paper to a reader other than herself, and the risk of prior ages of visionaries of nature's truer reality in faceless, mysterious beliefs better persuaded with the tactfulness of obsessive fear ravaging a history in silent, choking howls.

"The enigmatic pride of '*no mercy*' as an intention of will announces its illegitimacy of mercy as a sympathy of reflecting retort," she proudly wrote a few nights earlier.

Pondering the most soothing memories of her refamiliarizing childhood freshly encouraged by returning to the house, she controls herself best during instances imposing an encountering distraction of immediate challenge to steady her focus, such as a precariously risky endeavor, whether physically exuded like a climb or resisting the lethal instinct to run as a trait never held in common; or emotionally tightened strings of thought strafing the pressing actions required of an immediate, reckoning and proper feedback conferring upon her conducts from the invading frequencies of her environment as the teaching of identified belief.

The facet she saw in animals and nature while growing up here was the same as the intelligence of humanity in the city expressed through the designed abilities of moveable, actionable bodies with minds in communicative, insightful exploits within the unifying dynamics of reality, with all fighting for the recognition of newly perpetrating faces as the embracement of a notorious dread in the pains of a thick past enacted through ageless sacrifice.

She can see the displays of vision within nature's reenactments of salient past events, an ageless, whimsical artist and actor, a satirist and spectator.

"An unappreciated visionary before her time is nature!"

Signs of her childhood are everywhere the more she wanders and looks, as inexhaustible to seek out and rediscover as the rekindling symbols of nature, and her associating memories, links she has innocently written for her future self to recover from the environment surrounding her home, a game with herself across decades and into the future still to come with yet to be scripted, unread cyphers.

Walking her vicinity, the prior days, she found the wall of rocks still there from where she had placed them as a child, though mostly fallen away from the wall she once constructed with Henry's help and instruction as a collecting pool within the creek for her natural observations to find.

In some versions of an imagined, diverting future she would find cause to reconstruct it for the observation of other bright eyes to follow; but she also likes the idea of it still being from the past as the miniaturized ruins of a child's once proud claim over a small pool of nature as the hypnotizing magical lens for the encounter with science in the light of nature.

The broken wall with remaining stones submerged beneath the creek's cold, flowing, and crystal waters reminds her of his warning words with enough seriousness to stick in her memory, as important moments mostly would for later associated learning as far back as she remembers without anything before it, "what you are, who you will be, it will be uneasy for you, but you must never take on their blame as yourself, don't become as the victims of the stories you read."

Later, even recently and now, she questions where she would be, who and what she could have become as inclusive blame instead if not for her upbringing here, without the learned nurturing of two original strangers to adopt her, which could easily have been dissimilar as an alternative reality for her to endure and not appreciate later in its stead.

She keeps precious moments of her insertion within reality as far back as a point in her infancy in which she disappears from her own involvement, empty of her further interactions, and specific enough to claim as many individual clips of her life as if prior lives which can be pasted back together into a surfacing of one life and a current moment claiming new memories to associate with the future ones to cyclically come for her.

"This happens with the semblance of an eternity within one lifetime."

This is her practice, meditation, and transcendence of the waning moments, headwinds passing her as some instances a gentle rolling breeze and others a galling, swirling vigor occurring as the relentless tracks of time left behind.

They hadn't known what they were in for when they first arrived. There were many alternatives much less comforting than the one they offered her as a tough one to live for the betterment of its toughness. It was thrust as a surfacing contention between them as an uninvited predicament lacking the faith of its first intention.

She knows what she had found, in the nuances of carefully worded books, in the spirals of nature attuned to her coincidence of it, without fearful denial. No one proves such talents in the city where no one ever thought to look. She watched for fellow ownership and found a barren, dust-stricken, carnival landscape of unfocussed, mimicking wonderment.

Here is the only world she knows, the one they daily taught her, and her schooling. Homeschooled, the books she read were her only hints of another reality she rarely glimpsed otherwise, becoming for her imagination newfound symbols for her to escape her beachscape world to find in origination elsewhere.

~~

The first time she met a bear she must have been under ten years of age. She looked up and there it was, standing and looking at her from further down the beach, close enough she could make out the pointed ears and narrow snout with the nearest thing to lightness about it the faint glitter of teeth behind wetly dribbling, dusky lips and dark eyes too.

She didn't know what kind of monster it was, big and covered in black fur as dark as a crow, with its black nose sniffing the air for her scent breezing its way with the wind.

She didn't know its quickness or strength, or that if it had chosen to it could have pounced upon her before she had any chance to even get to her feet, not that there would have been a difference either way in the outcome.

From the trees behind where she sat alone on her stones, beforehand piling the flat ones in a towering statuesque-like shape resembling a stack, she recalled overhearing the birds in a frenzy and the shadows of many overhead gulls bypassing this way and that between herself and the appearing monster she sat helpless before.

Instead, the bear lowered its head, moving a few steps to a larger rock Sela couldn't have imagined picking up, and effortlessly turning it gently over with hard, blackly taloned stubs from a mighty paw.

For timeless minutes, the bear simply strutted about, never coming nearer to Sela, turning over huge rocks with the effortlessness of a giant until Sela, with each overturning rock, picked up a stone of her own and placed it atop her stack. Then, wobbling its backside back into the trees, it disappeared like a mouse in the leaves.

Later, she would see a bear on the beach

somewhere at least once a year, revealing to her as teaching no monster lived here; but the black bear could not teach her then the only beasts lied elsewhere as a possession wary of being spooked.

Those encounters seem a mere sentimentality to Sela now, even her precious memory of a mother bear and two cubs she spotted from her deadwood perch as they sauntered from the forest to the ocean shoreline. They appeared farther down the beach but close enough she watched the little ones tirelessly spin, tumble and twirl over each other for the longest time in downwind secret, watching them chase and become chased with the ebb and flow of breaking waves running up the pebbled sands of the shore.

The wolves were more secretive and harder to spot in the open beach. Sometimes, it was years between mere fleeting sightings.

She was within the trees, playing hide-and-seek with the birds, chipmunks, or anything else large enough which might spot her during a busy day. Sitting atop the soft lichen of a trunk felled many seasons before her arrival on the beach, covered in the multilayered freshness of new life as diverse shelter for many stages of tiny creatures and vegetations during its many years as a once tall proud tree slowly dissolving away into the forest floor like a cube of melting ice.

It was there, crouched in cover, Sela as a

mere child saw the wolf approach within her line of sight between the trees. It proudly carried the impression of roughened fierceness, though she had read them to be shy canine animals she might live to be fortunate enough to remember as a lucky gift if she ever saw one close, though she didn't think herself lucky caught in the moment, trying not to move as it smoothly cut a direct approach through the undergrowth.

Her face masked behind the broad leafy branch of a small forest shrub, the light suddenly broke through the cracked ceiling of the old forest, with a band cutting the shadow of the forest floor between herself and the wolf abruptly stopped half a rock throw away with eyes sighted upon her.

She sensed she had caught the wolf by surprise, sneaking as she had been doing among the trees as her quiet, blending way with her forest floor and encounter with it for that day's playground of reimagination.

Staring beyond the scruffy elongated snout, the dark, piercing eyes connected with hers for what seemed infinite split-seconds before the wolf just as easily looked to its left as if Sela weren't there at all and the two amazed sets of eyes had not met in mutually recognized surprise. Trying to take the stare away from her, it lowered its head to sniff the ground, then it bolted and was gone as if there was no surprise as all, tricking her an achieved prize.

She stood and walked out from her concealment behind the branch to try to spot it once more and yell so it would know they had met for real, that there was no taking away her gift of luck it owed her but running away as it did it wanted nothing more to do with her that day.

She remembered the wolf on her drive with Josh to the coast, holding the symbol taken from the house and not long before dropped off in an unstamped envelope to the apartment's mailbox in the city. A red, thinly metal flag otherwise broken and insignificant as nothing higher than penny scrap, the object she received a month before she had gone to the mountains with Josh for a retreat from her unease of it, and not long before she quit her job.

She had been playing with it on the drive back to the coast, knowing it to be the reason she was driving with Josh back to her home, and in retrospect the hinting reason she left her home to begin with without a return until then. She held the little red flag up to look at against the light of her passenger window while bringing it ever closer back to its proper, original place.

The red metal flag did hold a meaning to Sela and one other to send it to her as a symbolic challenge of eternal disagreement.

CHAPTER 6: SYNCHRONIZING FATES

The wet rocks softly wail beneath her steps on another of daily walks she takes weaving new paths over old ones throughout her vicinity like a spider inspecting and reinforcing her web. Lasting an hour or more each walk, she repeats the pattern a few times each day between her other chores and watchful feelings of things to come.

The true emergence of this awoken world, this newfound universe to smile at for a first instance as a time and place in unison like being locked in staring eyes with a hawk, she can't ignore as a permeating allurement of sensual implications and a mirror vision of identity to emulate.

The first day arriving home with Josh, she sidetracked herself to the old mailbox on a post centering the big rubber tractor tire fastened on the ground, once decorated with flowers now overgrown with long, thin grasses brown with age and dead roots. She removed the red flag from her pocket, placing it evenly and neatly back into its jagged fit as redundant proof to the urgency of its breakage by a hardened hand in her absence.

The object was sent as a private invitation to return home or live forever away under the depraved fear imposed by another's intimidating suggestion against her coming back.

Connecting the broken pieces physically together as she did, "the message has been sent, I know what comes for me here; translated as a simple form of consent in a depraved, untethered mind with thoughts like abscessed pains flinching to the softest touch."

Something new had been etched into the paint and into the depth of the metal itself by the careful rage of a shadow, *trancing* hand; a portending waning crescent moon with a short line underneath, Sela assumes, to mark as symbol the horizon over her ocean.

Sometimes, she studies other people seeing the signs of foreshadow like the feelings of love as the emanation of a famously named, idolized emotion which can't be withheld; instances when she absently holds a focusing sense for the igniting reflection of true colors much like the elucidation following a self-fulfilling act of bravery without the time permitted in the moment to think of the act, as if you didn't belong to the boldness taking hold of you as a fitting mood of disowning hindsight.

She absorbs the vibrations of these strangely impassioning reflections as inner invocations, as if they were her own emotions to experience through the illusory imitation of replicating a pure courage in choice; until she would see it less as people grew older, and sadly short-lived in the younger by an acute social contract of willful relinquishment; until these possibilities seemed not to exist at all except through the enthusiastic opportunities for chance to surprise her sightedness and make her involved, drawing her excitements by the poignant, coaxing metaphors afforded by her world through the hardening of time.

The multilayered symbol of a metal flag left for her gave her the eye-opening clue to everything and the inevitable best and only path forward as a final steadfast admittance to fearlessly live or perish by the will to overcome her willful agitator, the same one compounded globally throughout history; not hers alone, but her fixating version of it repeating as a new drama just for her hounding benefit and the bold requirement of her involvement, for her sudden and prolonging emotional response to occur, to agitate her fears and inhibit her thoughts into rash actions, to attempt to better and happily diminish her will at the hunger of those finding as uncorrupt the predatory spirit contorting the spirit of nature as the excusable origin of its artful, multifaceted, and reaching violence.

Before coming back to the coast, she

checked the date of the upcoming waning crescent moon, to be certain Josh would be gone back to the city days before its arrival so as not to cue his participation as a hero in a fitness deciding Sela's fate to privately own, and not his to become complicit through a partnership he might have been induced to offer.

She is cut off from the rest of the world, with no means of real access to trusting support as "the way it needs to be."

There is no one else identical in correlating sanctuary throughout the entirety of her past to accurately measure her now or during any earlier time of her life, except the one to poke at her with a flag and her surrounding world of nature picked as jurying arena to decide.

Like the child on the beach with the bear, she offers herself as sacrifice with the exposing aura of an impending fatalness by posturing the appearance of an easy mark with the scent of fear stronger than blood for a wounded, fawning doe fettered to a post, carrying as hopeless decoy through the entangling winds blowing over the locality the lure for the desperate howl of a wild, abscessing beast out of its mind in parched temper to closely approach.

In other ages, Ruth should have been considered a witch for her natural beliefs, as a fear, a rumor, and a superstition to magicless others less inclined to her intuitions, while imprisoned, drown or burned to instill a phobia-inspiring loyalty from the happily cheering crowds watching it while spreading its rumors throughout the countryside as the enablers of inhumanity's prime ruthlessness.

The reputation persists, even locally extending to her for those of a current world still conveniently embracing pitchfork valor for the justification of action appeasing to uneasy fears in need of handily placating for a better sleep.

"As a success, the old fears and superstitions of history hardly change over millennia."

Looking at the world around her for answer correlating to its past, Sela must assume, as a memory much like a dream pertinent to the present, the people around her now in her world are the same ones in other ages smilingly holding the literal and proverbial pitchforks and torches at the sacrificial image of her burning mother for her organic penchant for carefully plucked teas to drink and glad it isn't them on exhibit.

"Even the woman at the fruit stand might have a pitchfork in her closet just in case," rising a slight smile to her lips while coincidentally forgetting the woman's name.

The difference between the city and her coastal locality, like any spotted place anywhere else imagined in the world, is merely a difference in intensity of the compounding vibrations of exposure rather than a valid escape.

"There is no true, lasting escape," she admits while sounding pleading.

This spontaneous exile returning her back to home as a sole remaining sanctuary happens as an asylum for her staggering exhibition on trial, as a journeying wanderer of the beach endlessly in one direction and back again without advancement of time or the happening of change in the rest of the world in her absence.

She had begun achieving for Ruth and Henry what they accepted as what she wanted for herself, and then they died, leaving her as sole inheritance the beach homestead for herself to "try out for choice."

In the end, as the summation of points leading her life's path to her remote homecoming alone, escaped from a world "not to have my back," Ruth and Henry furthered her, as a life lived until now in welcoming exile, an alternative she wouldn't have been offered the same otherwise, a unique blend of multiverse extracted from the world of her origin, wherever it was she came from before they arrived as her agents of destiny, as a substitute chance she shoulders to be too harrowing a road of imagination to begin seeing as anything else properly better.

In returning and being here now alone, she

accepts the challenge of "*the arena*," the one-on-one of her adversary's preference and deliciously sided favor, intimidating the instigation imposed upon her in the choice of coming back home as an only means of reclaiming it as her true home.

"To not surrender an identity of myself in my world to the carefree, smirking claim of another."

With Josh gone the past two days, it leaves only five more nights before the night of the next date of the awaited waning moon. That is if she can trust in the expectable, which she can't and will need to be watchful for over the next days and nights the same as she has been the last two days and nights alone in and around the house since Josh left.

During the two weeks with him here, she was hesitant, but unless she met an abscessed animal in the trees out of its mind with the frenzy of pains, there was unlikely to be any incidence until she was freed as the silhouette of a doe crept unaware too near the taller grasses during a darkened night, without the safety of numbers and no clear sense for the nearness of her famished, impulsive foe.

~~

There are times when the streams of reality come at her in flash-flooding waves, whether seen through the rains or snows, the waters and airs, or the slow waves of a bleeding tree watched as a child through the cut veins of its excreting sap, staring at the real as it seamlessly balances with her vision and other senses of it, watching it materialize in light and slanted by gusting winds during a night's shadowy storm, appearing secret for her eyes to witness as arriving proof of its incarnation during a worldly epoch of otherwise impenetrable darkness surrounding her like the vast ocean surface she treads, and tempered in the glowing aura of relentless quenching into brittle light her submerging resistance to its drowning call.

"The prey must evolve to adapt anew, to reach into the delves of its striving components and find a solution to its predicament by whatever strain of emotive will it has to transform its world into something better, preferably omitting the originating predator at its core as a further risk to the prey's vulnerable status of order in its environment. This requires a purpose of resistance through the urgency of reading the impending, roaring change as the proper evolutionary will of an instilled vendetta," she willfully wrote since she got here as the description of a courage and reread it late in the noiseless night behind the lock doors of her remote home while awaiting the first light of dawn soon expected to knock.

Sela's emotional world of disheveled associations has grown in direct correlation to the roving, interrelated associations of reality, of evolution, life, of universal forces stuck to life, intertwined with it in true predicament of manifesting exchange. Accepting the risky dangers of a jagged world as the many pitfalls striving against individual life surviving the world while also threading its courage to tighter bonds within its discovery, the unaccepting risks are the ones imposed by corrupt wills beyond "a modesty of cope" in association to dishonoring actions.

"I might stumble off a cliff, or freeze to death lost in a subzero storm by the hand of my undoing, or drown at sea by my clumsiness, or drive myself in a frenzied, self-determining rage against the life proffered me as exchange, but I will not be the spiritual amusement for another, whether physically shaped in the prideful mask of a hollowed hominid, an animal, or a cosmic aspect of nature in its ethereal will to befuddle and deservedly trick," she determines as she words it best for paper in her thoughts beforehand.

The thing she learnt about living with humans, the same as in living with nature, "to never give away your fear, and especially never run," was the same advice she offered Josh in the mountains before they took a first hike in case they happened by chance, whether perceived as good or bad as lifetime destiny or luck, to come across the path of anything big in muscled posture and surface fierceness of appearance such as a cougar or bear.

"The moment you run from the challenge you become the prey by the conjoining admittance of your choice to be the one preyed upon by acting like it, except in ploy," she admits, deeming her saddening harmony with nature as akin to one fleeing the approach of a raging wildfire, confused in the panicked smoke and thrashing disorder until clear of its fury under the unsealing blue sky intensely fueling the strangling flames with its drought.

Living in the city, she has only found detachment from natural things, while for her it's different than it can be with strangers absent the memories of her sightedness from not having lived it and of unsound belief to reckon it as something other than "never missed," and urgently making of that reality for her nothing other than a private engulfing challenge to undertake to endure with suspicion and conflict, an emotional state not in harmony with her idea of her future in any place, "here or there," as she accuses both worlds as replacement for a biting self-infliction upon her feelings of guilt.

As an attachment worth her intimacy, the playground she felt and experienced here by the waters as a youth cut her too deeply to forget once in identifiable context with the rest of the world romantically alluded to in books and prewarned her by Henry as sympathy for her during his inevitable absence from her future, as a context disturbingly affecting her temperament with a contradictory bluntness she indulges as a mounting resistance to its trustful rule as one in demand of "standing against rather than hiding behind" as the goading motto of her individualism.

Everything she found in the city she finds in nature with greater emphasis and depth of origins. She recognizes there is no supremacy of humanity as a necessity to accept and live according to a new meaning "born from the pubescent frights in the undeniable abuse of humanity's ill-bred fears and unrelenting superstitions, and nothing more," she wants to whisper in the eternally dying ears of the fearful haunts in the night; instead, she writes it to paper on a new page.

"Humankind is a con, a grifter, and a thief," she adds.

To find the human spiritual being as an individual to aspire to become sadly meant being fulfilled enough to stand boldly excluded from it, to find a sole meaning in spite of it, to rebel and resist against its misrepresentations as a force of purpose; otherwise, to discard with it as an outdated thing, a spiritual loss and reborn replica, the pyre of the natural world as a roving sensitivity secret and unheard, mystical and unsighted as an alert prey in the urgency of actions, of unadulterated, purely enacted awareness skirting with the real surfaces of the living reality now "suffocated by the same chemical urgency as the slowly agonizing spiritual dissolve of a deathbed corpse," she didn't have the heart to write down in case of its possible hex of permanence.

She expects there should be cues, hints, reminders roused by the knotted world's mute, ghostly screeches begging for her to grasp the waves of reality signaling her eyes to see and her mind to correlate thoughts, perhaps nothing more worded than "hello" with its swiftly belittling "goodbye" soon following in untestable answer, and the loss of further relationship as scaling rebirth from an impending fresh reseeding impedingly due for the rising fertility of a post-scorched world; "so until much later" when a long forgotten time is remembered again as the source of its new awareness of it.

Narrowed to her own scale of survivability, a stranger has an advantage over her fixed in place by the house and the trust in her immovability, but she has her sense for reality to tell her observations of looming risk as a trust to keep in her skills with stringy foretelling, and a lucid sense for cunning the maneuverable textures of her world to her betterment with a confident belief tougher than brawn.

There is the chance of things occurring out

of sequence or imminently sooner. Truly, she is an easy target, a lethargic, limping prey announcing her readiness for sacrifice. The house is remote, and she is there alone. There are only the walks on the beach and through the forests she takes daily for signs of change and the emulations of intimate recoupling with a natural space she has forgotten, reenergizing her through the refreshing signs of her former strengths as an infant, child and teen.

There is a chance previsioned to reach her safely with minimal risk to a calculating intruder eager for a path to be open as the inviting paraphrase and extravagant translation properly implying "consent to any self-*abscessed,* bereft translator."

The first time, three years earlier, she had been unprepared, surprised by her lacking experience and not yet hardened of a properly enfolded distrust. Before that night, she had taken her presence for granted as the one missing out of an otherwise obscurity rather than the one with the sight to see a truer reality in its weave.

It is still a matter of waiting, feeling the ethereal silk of her web woven through the natural world encircling her home for tremors, being alert to the prewarning signs of an intention fixed upon and thereby reciprocally and unwittingly entangled with her in agreed contest.

~~

She finds the area of forest he had recently, within the last few days and certainly since the day she drove Josh off for the city, appeared and later disappeared.

Even with the red metal flag in her possession and the act of will initiated, the footprints in the sands near the wind-chiseled forest trees reveal to her a closeness for the realness of experience beyond the fantasies of imaginations, a sense for lethality not belonging to her alone, a kind sympathy from the waters, trees and rocks creeping into her flesh as a residual panic lingering in the air and the pebbles of the sands at the wretched candor of opposing sides, and as the stepping fruition of an initial canvas sketch coming alive with the augmenting layers of drenching colors.

She spots more of the same footprints in the sand atop the upward slope of the tide's peaking line a far distance down the beach from her home or an hour of slow sauntering. She follows them a long way up the beach, pointed out here and there in the sands between long swaths of stones until the steps swerve towards the tree line again into the forest nearer her home, shown to disappear and later reappear coming back the other way.

"He *enters* the beach back there," she whispers to the trees, for they are a man's print, not that she didn't know by now her premeditating assailant by name and local reputation the same as his younger brother once held it with him in common.

"Look at him, tall, confident in getting here, purposeful in his chosen direction, and there is only one thing here he came for, without sufficient effort or skill at concealment," she finishes, looking back at the long beach fading in the wake of her return to the house. "He's come once, preliminarily scouting, and he's been around before, so when will it be again?"

Her only indicator is the whispering etch of a waning moon foretold in the metal of a tiny red mailbox flag, with the date of the scheduled moon one more night away.

First one twirling oval-shaped shadow; then soon after, a second oval-shaped shadow cross the rocky beach in front of her path. She thinks of the shadows as floaters appearing randomly in her vision, as a lessening or swiftly moving absence of light flitting across the vision of a bright lit day, and a disturbance of easily recognized change much as her presence might be considered an absence or floater strangely appearing across the field of the beach's otherwise unobstructed way of seeing its world akin to the shadows of gulls across her field of vision as an impression of forewarning.

After she has gone a distance, wanting to look in the direction she came to decrease a regretful inhibition, she turns and begins to walk backwards as she continues her forward progress home, scanning the beach's length for any occurring alteration from when she saw it not long before.

In any attempt to portend for advantages the branches of future opportunities answerable to her present, Sela reassuringly knows with a sense of trust she must contend with the fact the future already knows what happens long before her pebble strivings for simple, trusting paths of gesticulating encouragement to follow.

The world is not here solely for her part as partial value to demand as she can due her deserving measure of will, but as something which must be found and thereby claimed alongside the enduring control of her will.

With no self-vision, she sought her reflecting answers within the textured canvas stroked with colored trickery by the deft musings of a roving master-instigator owned of the same wonderment as her, finding meaning with playful, toying dolls smartly dressed in the ephemeral colors of new styles of tweaked passions through plying imaginative scenarios of courage across eternity.

~~

The next night arrives promptly at dusk without the past repeating itself earlier than expected, and as the symbol of a mutually held significance between the reciprocal aspects of past and present as demanding resolution of conflict, while the impartial future merely peeks back as it always does, unless perhaps portending its own impending state as being at stake in the transpiring makeup of an eventful, risky reality to challenge as its past events to alter with a self-interest perking the curiosity of clever involvement.

"But the future, unlike the past or present, lacks permanence and is seldom at risk of becoming involved, for it always has the refreshing chance of another future soon following to await *its* resolution to come later," she admonishes, considering the future's predisposition to be much as the way of people traversing a present state in multitudes of histories.

Since she got back home, she hasn't seen any larger animals, no bear, wolf, eagle, and no hawk, just deer, and the smaller birds, but they unabashedly watch everything to go on anyway, keen for a thrill of twittering gossip and the excitedness owned of a voyeur's wretched curiosity, leaving her with an empty, portending feeling of desertion, as if her awaiting fate were not in fact the one she confidently envisioned when "still her resolution to come later" and not alone in the woods of a secluded beach with a crazed threat imposed upon her she has spoken to no one else about except through the whispering ciphers written in her notepads.

She leaves the house for the beach at dusk, with no reason this time to lock the door behind her.

With the red metal flag entering her possession, he has confessed his complicity to her, not provable by law, though "law has no place in this anymore, no begging or pleading, no asking for mercy," but solely by her discretion and as silently witnessed by nature, leading to these flowing moments she experiences now with a heightening sense of the interconnective network of all things in and around her beach much as the strings of her weblike wanderings around the area of her home stirring the assorted lives within it through the simple vibrations emanating with wild solicitude from her steps.

He admits his foreknowledge of actions to come against her mortal wellbeing with welcoming secrecy, leaving her no choice except to come home to commit the resolution her future demands of her, without recourse to anything or anyone else "for this to end."

Her premeditation is one of resistance to another person to proclaim to owe her harm in advance, and in doing so acting outside the bounds of law and under its protection from her as a cynical twist of reality imposed upon her from the urban world of laws and rules after the need of protecting herself, so for Sela it otherwise means, "who else?"

Even if he feels *just* in his mind associating himself with his perverting quest and fantasy for retribution, reparation, or the answer to the provocative question making his thoughts itchy, "he has the wrong feeling."

It was the summer with Cheryl, soon after she had left for her trip back the same as Josh recently left to return, leaving Sela here for the rest of summer to fend for herself as she asks.

They had taken a few public hikes available to the area, gone to roadside stands and small local gift or craft shops for supplies and browsing, and kept to themselves.

"There are no men for us here, trust me," she expressed before they left the city, so it was only them together at the house, spending days driving for the enjoyment of the natural sites and relishing lazy days, talking and laughing with the unburdening freedom of graduation behind them and a long expanse of oceanfront beach all to themselves for a few weeks alone to themselves.

There are a few books Sela read as a teen in which the author described journeys into the spiritual mysteries, higher realms, and otherworldly dimensions of contact associated with this loosely physical world, finding closer attachment through methods used to blend with these worlds in a way not noticeable otherwise in the waking state than by an inclusion of hallucinogens, usually through a form of peyote or magic-inducing mushrooms.

Considering herself a type of soldier of philosophy as a study and way of life, the same as an integrity of action, she had recently been hungry for its teaching outside the books she read.

She had spoken of these books with Cheryl at an earlier time, with her even reading a book Sela recommended, surprisingly finding it at the back of the University library. The conversations led to Cheryl finding a source for the kind of mushrooms described in the books through a trusting friend of a friend.

Cheryl, not having the same spiritual courage for odd adventures and contrary states of mind, not a student of philosophy but of business, wasn't interested in trying hallucinogens with her, but did get Sela a small bag containing three thin, dried and organic stripes affixed with plentiful green powder not resembling much of anything like a mushroom more than a stick of beef jerky looks like one, "if you're really sure," and she was sure for the time.

It was a risky journey which could lead to madness or death for the wrong pursuer, or so the books warned as obligation against the risks of false journeying by its readers and a harassment of the spiritual world spooked by too many unwelcome mushroom eaters.

Sela didn't want to harass the spirit world, but "simply visit it, have a look around to see, know how it feels like, and test whether it is all that bad as an otherworld or future to come. Then, I will come back," she thought with naïve self-persuasion.

She had chanced upon or associated with an old way of accepting and running with nature. In ancient customs and traditions, animals were means of communication with spirits of existence divulged through the filtering enhancement of hallucinogens.

She had gathered driftwood of varied sizes over days into a pile as fuel for a long-burning fire on the beach under the dark of a moonless night as accompaniment for her journey.

She finds the same pile of driftwood gathered over days awaiting her on the beach she reaches at dusk, with the same moon as then not due to arrive until the earlier hours of dawn following a long, dark night with its absence.

With the light of day exhausted, she sets aflame a smaller pile of dried woods surrounded in a circle of bigger, ash-tarnished rocks placed there long ago by another hand bigger than hers and being there as the firepit on the beach all along from her earliest memories.

~~

"Let me out," she yelled to the night, not out of the refreshing, enlightening physical high first soothing her, but out of her old reality as a shedding skin, finally out of its sobriety and into the plain world of truth.

"Let me out," she repeated with less urgency and a newfound wonderment for the sweet taste of her words, as a vibration akin to the flames and the smoke moved into swirls by her breath, with the light of night beyond arisen to her sights, and the dark of day released from the hidden folds of its embryonic reality slumbering since an earlier dawn of a long ago epoch, before the advent of human steps walking the stones of the beach, and long before any thought might have arisen considering the stones artful or of much practical use other than a cast aside deposit resembling a heap.

The flames highly raged as the effects of the one piece of mushroom she consumed in small bites with a tea earlier at the house had already long claimed hold of her journeying, so her steps circling the tall fire no longer seemed as her steps, and her steps didn't even feel as steps as much as a hovering just above a surface beyond the need for the exertions of walking.

She was no longer travelling alone, as the lascivious smoke and flames mingled with the disagreeing light and dark in eternal dispute, and as confirmation of her previous thoughts fixed to the spiritual otherworld of nature, animal, and lost souls, carnal shapes silhouetted as the drawings of cave walls flitted through her vision, but only on her peripheries so that when she turned for a closer look in disbelief it would vanish with new images appearing for her peripheral vision to focus, coaxing her to turn again as one led in a dance.

As close as the spirits came to her as she hovered her way around the campfire, looking upward to the starry night blurred by color for the solace of context, she wasn't afraid, and her body felt a sense for joy as a substance drunk by her breathing of air as natural as a fish in the ocean breathing without drowning from the waters to a depth of new darkness never penetrated.

Circling the fire in lost amazement and endless surrender, she danced with the spirit animals as more newly shaped animals, of peculiar kinds she had never laid eyes on before or imagined real, joined in the merriment as if a celebration or festival for one to arrive in awaited welcome.

One of the spirit beasts, shaped much differently than the rest, hovering like Sela on two legs rather than the customary four, broke through to her physical dimension outside her periphery with a rushed, leaping force knocking her to the stones and holding her pinned there with the heavy weighted rancidity and acidic burn of alcoholic exhalation closely filling her mouth and nostrils as the fumes of bile inducing vomit became locked inside her throat at the sudden pain in her body becoming a burning, aching pleasure choking her as she dryly, uselessly heaved to regain an urgency for breath not returning while a heavy, spirited beast pressed her deeper into the stones.

For a long timeless moment, Sela was utterly helpless, breathing as one drowning in water with gasping desperation as the man-spirit, appearing unsuspected on her beach from the physical world, groped at her with the swirling smoke of the fire suddenly bereft of animal anima from an otherworld joining her in dance, spooked away as a dissolving mist by one spirit intruding upon her circular journey.

Then, as brusquely as she was forced to the stones of her beach by the invading strength of her intruder, the impossible weight atop her was completely lifted off as the release of a burden complimenting an abandoning, unforgettable screech of terror she never forgot for its association with the air lost to her lungs and the cursing pledge of a different spiritual journey approaching.

Her first conscious breath coarsely spilled from her body with a spitting, coughing discharge, with only the screeches continuing as a fading away in the night, and with her ejected vomit on the stones and in the strands of her hair.

~~

This time, she spots her would-be assaulter appear within the faded edges of the light the other side of her raging fire.

For some, the seeming control of animals, and thereby the confidence to impart fear, can only come from the instilled sureness of holding a gun or a big stick, objects he would have laughingly predicted needing for Sela through the empowerment of his endowed *bigfistedness*.

She watches him standing waiting silently, as if inducing a fear in her by the mere sight of him here standing before her.

"Come closer," she yells, but he waits for the drama of not obeying her words, or perhaps perplexed by her standing there on the other side of the flames rather than running as would be natural to his hefty presence and intimidating arrival, "nothing to hide between us."

During the time here with Cheryl visiting, along the course of two weeks together, unrecognized to Sela, they had garnered attentions with the sufficient and base impetus to later take the long walk to her home after Cheryl was gone leaving Sela as suspect and alone.

This time, with the older brother, complicit in his obvious foreknowledge of his younger brother's intended act against her by being here now wanting to know the "how's and the why's" of what he suspects but doesn't precisely know about the sudden disappearance of his brother three years ago.

Her absent fear transfers to him in an act of desperation, the survival of the self alone as the instinct barring any empathy for a different confidence, making of him the prey of a truth revealed to the night and the universe as an authority to come.

She knows she has no explanation to give, no plead for understanding, no sympathy to reveal, and no trick to perform as she begins voicing her furious incantations not at the two-legged beast approaching closer to her fire, now courageously yelling his own appeal at her in the night as she loudly speaks her piece too.

Standing before this intimidation and all to come before, she stands before the universe too, before the waters and forests, the skies and stars, in accusation, demanding it to explain itself to her for such a monstrous thing to find confronting her in this private arena again, to have to be made to look across the fires at an alleged, instilled fear, "am I the one meant to run here?"

And her begging question for the universe to try to offer as reason in response, "am I merely your amusement here?"

"And is this yours?" In demanding pretext, she points at her would-be assailant, agitator, imitator, and murderer, while he in turn demands his answers from her by his right to know, for his idea of proper justice as a contorting of ideas, and the things he will do otherwise being the things he already has as the intention to do while he talks louder seeking the encouragement of her fear as betterment to rally his impulsive spiritedness into action similar to how alcohol might also work as it pulses an aligning context of justification through his veins.

They have made a half-circle of walking around the fire she kept at a raging height through the night as beacon for his approach and so he wouldn't miss her or be surprised.

The ocean is at her back, and the forest to his back as they face across the flickering sparks and eddying smokes of the fire carried into the dark to quench and disperse.

She feels the first drops of a light rain

speckle her face as there appears from the night what she believes in anticipation will appear in one form or another, the sudden glare of canine eyes showing from the smoke and the dark of the beach into the light of the fire as an occurrence bringing with it an emerging smile from Sela at its self-actualization; but what she expects to see, he is shocked to see.

Then, a second pair of glaring eyes appears from the other side, and more as the entire pack of five appear from the dark of night into the edging light of the flames.

With a lingering smirk to her intruder as her show of fearlessness, she plucks but a petal of his terror to feel as the smallest yang of her compassion finally found through his impending undoing as she calmly turns away from him to face the ocean and sit atop the stones of her beach with crossed arms to await the rise of the moon.

Behind her back, as if by cue of a stage role actor, knowing by the grinding sounds of firstly a mere few stones overturning, he runs, and then as so many stones overturning at once, the pack pursues.

~~

"It's a dirty thing to have to do, a filthy game

to be cleanly made to play," she wrote a few nights earlier knowing the only context for the words are in her mind to betray her, and to whom there is no one else to explicitly trust with it as her accepting future lot to reap in punishment, "if such a thing is called for beyond a properly natural justice by outcome, harkening a duel of antiquated, overromanticized ages as an archaic battle to the death."

Digging the hole deeper, pushing the shovel with her booted foot harder through the sandy earth beneath the stones she had earlier cleared away, she expects no karmic rebalance sowed in cathartic entanglement to her future.

"The release is now," she freely believes, "this is the catharsis," while dually exposing the emotional shift of her beach world for a different, future, other world likewise freed from the distressing pair of assaulters; instead, in common encouragement, to endlessly, helplessly haunt the trees and waters of the ocean shoreline with "no mercy for release," associating such callous disregard of kindness in the physical world its true sentence of coming redemption in the spiritual one existing alongside it in charm, tortured as the eternal pickings for the amusement of birds.

With the first brother, she expects it was a bear by the force to pull him off her, and with the extensive slashing of his body she saw in the morning light when she got up from the stones and first stepped away from the dying embers to discover his body atop the stones of her beach.

Emptying her shovelful of sandy dirt, she stands within the hole, testing its depth to near her shoulders, as she continues digging the hole, "not an easy chore to do" she recalled ahead from her firsthand experience years earlier, and so she began to clear the stones and dig the ground the day after Josh left for the city in eager anticipation of a future mourning.

"He's a fat one, I have to go deeper. I don't want him later floating up through the rocks," with another second wind encouraging her in the early light of a briskly reviving dawn.

Through the countless ages of humanity, and even more the longer withdrawn into the past she ventures to conceive, there must have been others to find this dangling vine of attachment with an oddly reconfiguring world. She couldn't be a first to experience this manifold natural realm as an essential, undeniable experience alive with fused temperaments. These facets she shows herself as witness within the textured reality of the world existed as a diversity of natures of which she is a mere somebody joined in this sightedness through the temporal accident of having spotted it in common.

Late in the morning, while descending into the ocean waters from the shore to cleanse the prior night's filth from her skin, hairs and clothes, wildly refreshed by the cold, bitter wetness, she can feel the extent of the entire oceanfront threshold as a deeply dimensional dignity surrounding her. The entire image of the beachscape alive in her mind can be mutually reached into and touched by her fingerings of it through the forces pushing back and giving the interrelationship to her sensory attachments by its fingering probing of her as the searching touch of the blind for higher meaning of an unsighted world felt as the surfacing colors smearing an otherwise darkness.

She is forced to recognize what had been missed by the distracted multitude throughout the history only after perceiving the world to be an esoteric lesson of the few brave enough to sight it.

She appeared a vulnerable victim, a pawn and easy target, "a favored prey filling a vacant niche in the longstanding folds of human history's dishonor in choosing the accentuating advantages and easy absolution of running away from a fear while reciprocally in karmic balance embellishing the empowerment of another to instill it."

Each brother had looked as someone might in the medieval histories rightfully pummeled through vigilante stoning by a vindictive mob of bloodthirsty jurors as plainly sighted, bled cure for the viciousness of all sins.

In prior epochs of nature, the old and sick animals were taken not for mercy, but due to abundance and a kind of sympathy for the original sinful choice of flesh for energy without regard for an inevitable emotional future filled with varied and clever nuances rather than simply looking for following the sustenance of a meaningless permanence to life.

The predator of nature is primarily one of need not indulgence as corrupted by human ingenuities and the unavoidable opportunities available the unmatured histories of a growing infantile and pubescent consciousness.

Like two siblings out hunting, the older teaching the younger the strategies endorsing the alleged instinctive paleness of a disparaged prey as the predatory ease of conscience, they hone together with conjoint encouragement the obligatory, practicing skillset of a predator stalking its unwary prey.

With this twist of predatory edge transposed from reality into the witting advantage of self-imagined landscapes of fantasy assumed from the alleged tattered garbs of blind, stumbling vertigo concerning the natural world, these dizzy, malformed temperaments are best eschewed from the world as outside the reproaches of sympathy due the longstanding harms needed in rebalancing the world from their aims.

"I can do it too in kind," she freshly thought as a first idea to come to her in connection to its emerging reality within her awarenesses, to enter that bullying world as "its aggressor and intimidator bearing a will stronger than the physical with its towering obesity and collapsible shape like origami reshaping a sheet of paper into a miniaturized chickadee."

Sela could stand on a cliff face somewhere with no one to find her, and the risk of life her choice to make with a single last leap. It might be a bypassing crow, a deer, or far-off howl stinging her ears to break her from a mesmerism and alternate reality of fate.

Remembering the woman on the platform, the crossing fates existing as impulses through the veins of an urban landscape, an acting body with ample niche opportunity for parasitic successes to rove dressed in the furs of predators they've never slain to take, plying an easier mark as a favored prey in the cold eyes of a heavily muscled beast chilled by the naked fear of its unalterable stance.

The woman might have felt Sela's presence, as instinctive senses will sometimes tell without directly perceiving it. Such emotions were hindering without the accumulation of its practiced sights into an intimate icon of belief. The association she fixes between the dual incidents on her beach, each ending neatly concealed beneath the stones of her remerged beachscape, and the strange woman on her platform is an uninvited meaning imposed upon her from the designs of nature.

Sela has the words to try to explain a configuration of reality to a strange woman on a ledge pondering her fate in the middle of the night, but her attempt was as likely as not to be too honest in unsympathetic texture to stop the other woman from stepping into the abyss as a better alternative of pursuit and a fresh start simply due to Sela being there differently and urgently for her.

In fact, the woman might have been saved or her path altered by the simple act of Sela's wordless coincidental attention suggested her by the unbeknownst, impending moment. These coinciding instants compelling her intentions also fed her later guilts due to her alleging role in its outcome, whether she ever learned it or not, instilling a preference for learning over not knowing for its lessening of uncertainty, even if whatever drew her didn't really belong to her as a choice made by her innermost will to act a mere difference as surrogate for true value in other eyes.

Within the driving intentions of dominant posturing and bulkiness, he had thought her as exposed, vulnerable, weak, and wrongfully freed. He acted on that intention easily predictable to Sela as an empty pride of stature, on his idea and proving belief of her as "less than him on the pound-for-pound scales of his cosmic measurement," without the full comprehension of the scaling differences of perspectives motivating the world around him beyond a convenience in size.

None of the flesh was taken, like a tainted, poisonous meat, with only the fullness of spirit energized through the consumptive act itself and carried away for further satiating of dry thirst.

She only has the strength of her "convicting belief in the proper balance outcoming without prayer, and no alms, at least not from me to be cursed with later by debt."

She remembered the first time she had clawed the earth with her hands to dig the hole in her fresh rage illuminated by the new morning, with her hands covered by the filth of the earth.

Later, she went to the house for a shovel.

This time, she had a shovel ready in a premeditated urge for better preparedness. Days before, she had dragged to the beach and left in the trees a large wooden wheelbarrow specially made with an oversized wheel, crafted by Henry for Ruth's beach collections many years ago and still practical to use, to float swiftly over the stones even with a heavier load.

"The multiverse idea is vague, if you've heard of it, but it's the universe of the future not the present or past. It's the experience of living and it's something more people should be cautious of, since it finds its impending permeance, like the hardening of stone, from the marked verses of the past. It can easily revert, among individuals, as it's plain all over the world to historically see with the nearing turn of the counted millennia, into a private dissolution of extreme consequences."

"I haven't heard of it. I'll check it out when I get back," Josh had spoken with a keenness he always showed in listening and letting her know he listens, even if he had no intention of remembering to check it out later.

She has come to believe her fate not her own. She has been created, regulated, and cheated by a refined variation of genetics used to favor nature, to act in mutual attention of *her* interests. She is made to perceive in ways others appear unable, confusing her younger years with a growing sightedness she didn't fathom others as not having the same as her, and thereby malignant as a tumorous personality.

Henry had told her, "as the protagonist of your story, the same as each is theirs and this is mine, you must prepare to act against those who will wish to do you harm, for you can't count, as in a book, on the expectation that a hero will rescue you in a coming page or chapter. In fact, in the tales of the stories of their lives, others will often tell you to make it a part of your continuing story that it is not for your benefit to write it for yourself.

"Author your story yourself, don't let others

write it for you. And never let anyone make you a victim and minor character in *their* book, for most aren't good books worth reading."

She could stay here alone, in the house on the beach, but what would it be following years and decades of being able and perfectly capable to stay here alone. Who would she be then? And what does it say of that capability as a preference to the rest of the world?

Such sacrifices have been made before, in other times and locations of this roving spectacle.

A natural connection resembles her notion of a sensitive, unrequited love which must be selflessly claimed as both real and magical in mutual enchantment and wonder. A wonder spoken for her reciprocal to her speaking for it in wordless exchange, neither ever certain if the other is truly real, or to be believed or faithfully followed with trust as person, nature or city, or as a converging catalyst tempting the world of change, of trying and not yet succeeding in endless progress over millennia of ceding witnesses living new lives of doubting sightedness.

In getting here, the stomping vibrations of even a stealthy intruder are quickly heeded by the trees and animals through a gossiping interrelationship of manifold curiosity. No one could pass to the weblike center of her secluded beach homestead without being detected as suspicious and alert to watchful eyes as a menacing spirit not much different than a ghostly-lit apparition might appear to the human eye as a foreboding aura surrounding another person.

In the distance, over the horizon, storm clouds are inching closer, an unsurprisingly good sign giving Sela the elation enough to broadly smile.

"A good heavy rain will properly cleanse the beach," she thinks.

In the moment, she has no further reason to leave, or to run, or to fear. For what feels and is a first time in years, she has no place else to be, no predictions, no plans, no watching for the signs of prewarning her reality ahead in practice.

The coincidental elation from her smiling at being freshly alive under the warm morning light on her beachscape, vigorously absent further feeling or focus of callous intent specific to her during her flowing instant under the warming ocean winds, is the freedom of her typically unflustered universe taking note with extraordinary harmony to Sela's journey, emulating with kindly gifting imitation her modest reshaping of her future.

The End

ABOUT THE AUTHOR

Rayne Corbin

From Canada, and a graduate in Information Systems, Rayne Corbin styles a systemic view of nature and human reality.

His writings explore the philosophical challenges instinctively surfacing from the active and intricate tendencies of a creative existence.

Rayne Corbin (pen name used by Chris Handrahan)

BOOKS BY THIS AUTHOR

Involved Interpretation: And The Inevitable Evolution Of Resistance

"Involved Interpretation" is a book of five essays about the created environments and perspectives of the world. Two recurring themes are: the misrepresentation and loss of environmental meaning through humanity's dividing impulses for dominance as a defining measure of success; and the misuses of the origins and symbolic depths of evolutionary feeling and thought experienced through the world's living beings including humans.

The book explores how this misuse of original symbolic understandings is advantaged through the exploitations of beliefs initiating from a shared, convergent misreading of the environments of reality and the proper emotive meanings of its thought-inspiring symbols as they have been found in the world, claimed and collectively gathered as ownership throughout human history to a present world.

Spectrum Of Depthless Enthusiasm: And The Instinctive Challenge Of Integrity

As an encouraging change to an interpreted mythology, "Spectrum of Depthless Enthusiasm" looks at the old world through the inverse focus of aspergic interpretations on the designs of premeditated, personality- and fear-persuaded physical and mystical experiences, to shine a brighter light and better color the nonmythical lives quietly hidden in plain sight.

With provoking narratives to relevant, urgent themes, "Spectrum of Depthless Enthusiasm" illustrates the differences of association and empathy the aspergic identity constructs of the world in the face of neurotypical determinations, as past and present surreal influences forced by coinciding involvement to contest for a truer experience of an otherwise natural world.

The Disciplines Of Time: Survival Of The Fittest?

"The Disciplines of Time" looks to the past, science and nature for descriptions to the present systematic predicament of a planet and a clear forewarning for the future.

These essays provide motivating ideas and creative perspectives on a range of topics for the encouragement of attention, such as the complexities of evolutionary niches, the cleverness of light, the sensitivities of a natural world bound by the rules of relativity and the quantum arena for solutions, the paradoxes between personalities, the gameplaying stratagems of disinformation versus information, the first causes of resistance and dissent, and the opportunities afforded by original inexperience upon the fitness of a future world lived in a current state as an unkind, unsolicited reflection of the past.

It is a book on the success and failure of systems, the influences of time, and the fateful beginnings of belief excavated from natural symbolic meanings as first communications between a natural world and its progeny.

"The Disciplines of Time" is comprised of 10 essays combining in whole two previously published books, "Involved Interpretation" and "Spectrum of Depthless Enthusiasm."

The Disciplines Of Time: Illustrated Edition

Illustrated Edition includes 22 color images of Canadian wildlife photographed and selected by the author.

Printed in Great Britain
by Amazon